A KID
FROM
THE
BRONX

Norman Weistuch, Ph.D.

PAGE PUBLISHING, INC.
New York, NY

First originally published by Page Publishing, Inc. 2017

ISBN 978-1-63568-781-1 (Paperback)
ISBN 978-1-63568-782-8 (Digital)

Printed in the United States of America

ACKNOWLEDGMENTS

THERE ARE MANY PEOPLE I would like to thank who contributed greatly to the development of this book. First and foremost, I am close to the members of my immediate family and would like to thank my wife, Janet, who, through our share of ups and downs, has never wavered from her love and support. To my children, Corey and Jessica, who are both in college now (my son in grad school and my daughter a sophomore), I cannot say with enough love and devotion that they have made me proud beyond my wildest dreams. I owe a special thanks to my son Corey. As I was writing a book that was fictional in nature, although with a psychological emphasis, he suggested that I shift gears and write a book consistent with my own experiences; and without his refocusing my thinking, this book would never have come to be.

To my friend Mark Steinman, who grew up together with me in the Bronx, I am thankful for his friendship and caring about me and my family, and I would especially like to thank him for feedback about the earlier stages of this book.

With grateful appreciation, I would like to thank Allison Williams for her support and contribution to this project. Her willingness to help and to be interviewed for this book has been a great boost to my hope and dream to complete this project and get a strong message out to the public.

Of course, I cannot thank enough those individuals who offered their time, patience, and cooperation to provide interviews about their own life stories without which this book would not have come alive. As I am bound by my promise to you that I would keep all identifying information confidential, I can only say thanks, and you know who you are.

The historical portions of this book embed all I am saying in a true and concrete framework. I have already thanked those who contributed to the writing of my doctoral dissertation. As it pertains, however, to this current volume, I cannot thank enough the following people:

To Nicholas Lemann, formerly of the *Atlantic Monthly* and currently on the journalism faculty at Columbia University, I owe him a debt of gratitude for permitting me to use large portions of his two-part series about the war on poverty.

To Gregory Kornbluth of the staff at Harvard University Press, I thank him for his cooperation in asking Daniel Matlin for his permission to use large portions of his article in the *Harvard University Press Blog* about the unknown Kenneth B. Clark. A debt of gratitude is owed to Daniel Matlin for granting his permission for its use.

I also greatly appreciate the help and feedback of Steven Herb, education and behavioral sciences librarian at Penn State University, for his feedback about the use of my dissertation for this current manuscript. He was also invaluable in connecting me with James McCready, to whom I owe my gratitude for correctly researching and listing the citations for this book. Steven also introduced me to Brandy Karl, who is a copyright officer and affiliate at the Law Library at Penn State. I thank her as well for her feedback about copyright law and the use of my dissertation for this book.

CHAPTER 1

THIS IS NOT A BIOGRAPHY about me. It is, however, about a range of experiences I have had that is worth sharing; and my background, the time I was born and raised, and the career I have chosen have all contributed to decisions I have made and observations and experiences I can talk about.

I was born in 1953 and grew up for the first twenty-four years in the Bronx. New York City is a busy and exciting place, and the ethnic mix in New York has allowed me to experience the wealth of many cultures that make up the fabric of the city. People had grown weary after World War II and were glad to move forward and see the United States as the thriving place of opportunity it had become. Technology and labor-saving devices were all the rage, and housewives had more time on their hands but were there every day when their kids came home from school. It was a different society in which I grew up than what we see today. However, there are cultures that have not been so fortunate; poverty is seen nationwide, and this has never changed dramatically.

It always amazed me as a child that you would go into New York City and you would see skyscrapers and many exciting restaurants and a culture of wealth. However, you could drive three blocks away to pockets of poverty where there were old buildings, people with open liquor bottles, prostitutes, and piles of garbage in the shadow of the wealth I have just described.

Culture has always been an ethnic mix in the city, and poverty will target certain groups at different times in our culture, groups who receive the butt end of life. As my parents grew up, the Jews were targeted, and religious prejudice and prejudice against East European traditions were noteworthy. If there were signs in the South saying "No colored," in New York City—and I am sure in other places— there were signs during the Depression, when jobs were scarce, stating, "Jews need not apply."

There has always been an unwritten code, if you will, that in these experiences, there is some commonality between Jews and other ethnic groups and cultures. This goes back as far as the days of the Henry Street Settlement House on the lower east side of Manhattan, where wayward Jewish boys from the streets had a place to come and play basketball and had a better shot at life. Social workers, many of whom were Jewish, began to have a sensitivity to what their parents and relatives went through and began reaching out to offer their help to those in need.

My father was one of those growing up on the lower east side of Manhattan during the Depression, and his parents had settled on the lower east side, having emigrated from Poland. There were tenements back then—rundown buildings with one bathroom on each floor and bathtubs that would be covered over with a wooden plank and double as the kitchen table. I remember seeing my grandparents as a child. When I was very little, they still lived in one of the tenements, and as I got older, they were all torn down and replaced by low-income projects.

As we walked to their home, we could smell urine in the subway station and on the streets. There was an odd mix between these odors and the odors of food vendors on the street as you would walk down Delancey Street near Orchard. It was a mix of stores for inexpensive homemade garments, food, and the like and foods as well from places like Puerto Rico, Cuba, etc. The culture that had for many years been singularly Jewish was beginning to become a mixture of both Eastern European and Latin American cultures.

The early 1960s brought a strong level of hope about America, and with the election of John F. Kennedy, the world of Camelot was seen on every TV screen in the nation. It was then a nation of hope, which was about landing a man on the moon, sending volunteers into third-world nations through the Peace Corps and even local programs such as Vista to help the disadvantaged in this country.

However, the politics of this nation proceeded, and it was a small contribution in a well of despair that was impossible to cure.

John Kennedy and Jackie came from enormous wealth, and they did not really comprehend the have-nots in a way that could really be of much assistance. However, the time was right for the public to have to respond to inequities that would move the society we live in forward in significant ways. Desegregation was the law of the land and would have to be enforced. This led to two divergent paths to make these issues clear to the American public. Dr. Martin Luther King followed the path of nonviolent resistance and instructed the black community to stand up for its rights and the law, which meant that people of color could ride buses in the same way as any other passenger and not be forced to sit in a separate section at the back of the bus. This led to nonviolent boycotts in Selma and elsewhere in the South. People were hurt in tangles with the police for boycotting, but eventually the laws were enforced and these rights were preserved. The other path advocated by Malcolm X and the Black Muslims was a violent one and led to riots, looting, and many behaviors that might have brought attention to the problem but in a way that created more negative pressure and negative stereotypes.

As the 1960s raged on, the Johnson administration set the ground rules for the war on poverty and the most ambitious period of legislation to pass through Congress since the Roosevelt administration and the Great Depression. This included the voters' rights legislation, which prohibited blocking blacks from voting by ridiculous standards, such as remembering portions of the Constitution, laws enacting Medicare and Medicaid, and the birth of the Head Start Program.

I entered elementary school local to my home, and by 1962, there was a dramatic change. As I have already started talking about the happenings related to desegregation, I can personally talk about my experiences with desegregation as I entered grade 4 in the New York City Public Schools. There was an uproar, as in this year, desegregation was enforced, and black and Latin American students from schools in the South and East Bronx were bused to my local school (in north Bronx). It is a sad commentary on how people responded to it. There were older teachers at my school, and by September of my fourth-grade year, they either resigned or took early retirement, and younger teachers were rapidly hired to take on the changes. Another despicable occurrence was that many more parents before the start of that school year decided to put their children in Catholic or Jewish parochial schools to "avoid the blacks."

Although there were only about five or six students in each class, the differences were noted, and for students like myself who grew up with students of color, it was much easier in my opinion to see them as other students in your class and just other kids. There were misinterpretations by young Jewish liberal teachers, however, such as the following: When I was a fifth grader, I was chairman of a committee report for social studies, and a girl my age who was of color was on the committee. My teacher yelled at me for being prejudiced as I gave her a more minor role, which I thought was being considerate because she lived far away and had no way to meet with me or the other kids after school as she would go home on her bus at the end of the day. The teacher thoroughly confused me. Although it did not for me, this could have created anger toward someone who caused me so much trouble with my teacher and might have had that effect on some kids.

What has always troubled me is that you can change someone's environment, but you do not always change the influences that affect a person and make them who they are. It is up to each individual to form their own basis for motivation. However, it is certainly better to begin to modify the environment so that forces have more chance to take root in becoming part of someone's experience. Not everyone who grows up poor, however, is going to be a drug addict, a dropout, or a thug. This is especially poignant now as we sort out our immigration policies about those from the Middle East, as not every Arab is a terrorist, and certainly, the Muslim faith, as is true of most faiths, is based on peace, not on war or terror.

Unfortunately, as I will speak up many more times about financial and social inequity, the current system of public assistance and Medicaid creates a surefire way to failure. As has always been true of most social service programs by the government, they are poorly funded. Although you cannot let people go under and the program includes housing assistance, medical assistance, financial assistance, etc., unless the motivation of the individuals is to get off public assistance, most of the people I have met on public assistance are drowning.

There are many instances of men who are constantly unemployed and underemployed, brought up on drug charges, are in and out of jail, etc. These individuals will do better if taught how to break the cycle of poverty. The cycle of poverty is not broken by the politicians but by each individual given the opportunity to learn and experience success through a different path. Otherwise, the stereotypes continue, and the police continue to become brutal to people who scare them in poor neighborhoods where they are "taking their lives in their hands" and reacting in over-the-top ways to brutalize and "handle" the public. It is well-known that the justice system is biased against people of color, but the system is not set up to help as much as to keep down those who are reacting in frustration and despair.

The label of "welfare mothers" has been applied to those who have tried to raise families on public assistance. With the absence of fathers in most of the families where this label is applied, it has become a label to stereotype a whole group of people who are considered lowlifes and people who, in even thinking about them, breed contempt from those with greater financial resources. It is one of the strongest arguments that is offered about entitlement programs. *These are not people who are entitled.* They are more forced into a system that, like everything else organized and run by political bureaucracy, perpetuates itself. Generations of mothers raise children who continue the pattern into their own family life as they mature and have their own families raised on welfare.

Some programs started in the 1960s have been more successful than others, for example, Head Start. The beauty of a program like Head Start is the fact that the children involved are started very young. The program provides a free preschool education to those under the income guidelines who qualify. I have my doctorate in school psychology from Penn State University. Although to preserve anonymity, I will not say where my first job was as special services coordinator for a large Head Start Program.

Funding was always an issue, and the salaries for the staff at the program were incredibly low. I had the idealism and the youth to offer my services at a low salary for a period of time. Some of the staff were of the same mind, including teachers and other coordinators like myself. Others, however, were less well trained, and I cannot speak to trends nationwide but clearly, as will be offered many times through this book, lack of funding to an underserved population will inevitably lead to a lower success rate. However, there were many excellent things that happened in this program and throughout the nation, I am sure many idealistic individuals who have contributed greatly to the growth of preschoolers and their families.

One of the unique things that are part of the design of Head Start is the degree to which there is parent involvement. This has an excellent side, which gives the population of "welfare mothers" an opportunity for learning and training that provides motivation, a boost to self-esteem, and a chance to have impact on the growth of their children. Women worked in the classroom and took parenting classes, and for some, there was a program provided where you could take CDA classes and become an assistant teacher; and those parents who entered the program often came from the ranks of parents who were motivated for a better life for themselves and their children. A parent/staff board was involved. This input has a positive side, but there must be great care in how this is handled, because there is a false assumption about parents running their own program, which cannot be stressed enough. The input is fine so long as it is managed by trained professionals who can turn the ideas into practical solutions. As long as parents are open to feedback and willing to learn, this works out well.

There was a wonderful staff and many people who contributed to the growth and development of this program. I not only had my training at a high level of psychology to offer the program, but I was still connected with the university. Use of technology and programming from the local university is a model that is applied in many areas of the country, beginning at demonstration schools and preschools on university campuses across the nation and reaching out into the neighboring communities.

Secondly, the education coordinator of the program was the spouse of a minister in the local area. As I talked about earlier with the social service movement including such unique programs as the Henry Street Settlement, there had been a long history of Jewish and Christian social services movements, and often there was money raised to this end by the Federation of Jewish Philanthropies and Catholic Charities, for example. The education coordinator had a forward-looking view to the development of the program and had this unique vantage point connected to her background with her church and her willingness to advance the program and listen to feedback in many practical ways. She was also a well-trained educator and brought this to the table as well in terms of management of the program. The third person was the director of this Head Start Program, who was originally a trained teacher who taught high school in the local school district before taking on this position.

However, a key obstacle to the success of Head Start Programs was the original design from the federal government. Head Start was embedded in a larger social initiative, which made it harder for Head Start to achieve success. These programs were referred to as Community Action Programs, and although the intent involved help with bills, such as the power bill, rental assistance, etc., the administration of these programs meant that the heads of such programs determined where the funding went, including to the local Head Start. The director of our program, like others in similar situations, initiated a political battle to separate administratively the Head Start from the Community Action Program. He was victorious, and the Head Start funding was then channeled directly into the program.

Another thing that is a flaw in the design of and operation of many Head Start Programs is the fact that even though the larger program is managed in each county, space in each local area is often rented in local churches, etc. This makes the program cumbersome and hard to administer. Thinking as a conventional educator, the director of this program bought an old school building from the local district, and all the Head Start classes became based in one building, with a more conventional bus system to transport the kids, and the program now could function as an integrated school. All the unit heads, the director, and the classes were based in one place.

The program functioned like a family environment with many parents there during the day doing various things for the program, including making decorations, participating in classes such as parenting classes, helping in the classrooms, etc. One of the things I remember most fondly, as I am a food lover, was three grandmotherly individuals who had a kitchen available to them and cooked wonderful homemade food for the kids and staff at no cost to us. Because I was one of the few men in the program, they would load my plate up with as much as I could carry to give me a good breakfast and lunch every day. With the fractured families that were characteristic of many of the kids in the program, this gave them a sense of family—meals, grandmothers doing the cooking, and life experiences they could cherish as they developed.

Another thing that added to this sense of family was a concept that was often seen in reverse currently in nursing homes, where young children are brought to the nursing home to play with grandparent figures, and it is therapeutic to both. At the Head Start Program, we had foster grandparents in each classroom who helped the teachers and kids and gave that sense of having grandparents in each and every classroom. At a later time during my two and a half years with the program, about 10 percent of the two-hundred-plus children in the program could be classified preschool handicapped. This meant that in addition to receiving speech services if needed, they could receive special education services in the community (OT) and other needed services including a split program where they could spend half the day at Head Start and half the day in a preschool handicapped class provided by the special services offered in the area. We also were permitted to write IEPs, or individualized education programs, which spelled out educational goals and objectives for students who needed special learning opportunities to develop and grow properly. I was given permission to train the foster grandparents to implement the IEP goals with individual children, and this was a good use of their time.

There were several other things that happened in the program that were noteworthy contributions. One of the big debates that I had with the education coordinator was around the choice of a curriculum. Many Head Start Programs do not function, as is true of preschool programs in general with certified teachers and with all the educational technology that is seen in a standard school program.

The argument was about the type of curriculum to implement. Many people believed that Montessori curriculums gave the children opportunities to make their own choices about what they learned, hence motivating kids to be invested. However, in my own opinion and when I checked with others at Penn State, the other side of this is that kids from impoverished backgrounds tend to be more overwhelmed by having to make such choices, and when the curriculum is far more structured, it creates a better learning situation. We finally chose the more structured curriculum, and with it, there was a testing program to place the kids where they were developmentally in reaching the curriculum goals.

So as not to be misunderstood, I would like to add that contrary to popular belief, Montessori curriculums are highly structured so that if a child chooses a certain area of the curriculum to explore, the steps to get there are highly structured, but the child still needs to make the initial choice, which was not required in the curriculum we went with. The director authorized me to work over the summer, along with two teacher aides, to bring kids in and test all the preschoolers in the program before implementing the curriculum in the fall. We got through this and had to be creative, as many of the parents did not have cars or were not reliable about keeping appointments, and we went to pick them up at their homes so we could keep a schedule and complete the testing program over the summer.

The curriculum went off beautifully, and this was a great success. Other things that were positive outcomes related to my interest in transition from preschool to public school and after consistent pressing of the local school district, they finally agreed to send their kindergarten teachers to observe our preschool classes, and we sent our teachers to observe the kindergarten classes, making it easier to smooth the road for the kids about what to expect and for the kindergarten teachers to have a better handle on the kids they would receive the following year.

What I was also able to offer has been a valuable program begun at the university level and applicable to use with young children in many working situations through my career. Two faculty members originally from Rutgers University in New Brunswick, New Jersey, were a husband-and-wife team. They developed a collective training and therapeutic model referred to as relationship enhancement. Drs. Bernard and Louise Guerney developed the use of listening skills as a mechanism to enhance couples' relationships as well as parent-child relationships. These skills can be taught. With young children ages two to ten, it is possible to conduct play therapy sessions, which give kids who are younger a chance to express their feelings through play as they do not often have the verbal skills to benefit from talking therapy.

I had the good fortune of being at Penn State after the Guerneys moved there from Rutgers. Louise Guerney was my mentor in learning these skills. There was also a parenting skills sequence, and I had the opportunity to see kids who needed therapy at Head Start to conduct play sessions with these children, conduct parenting skills training (although there were other such courses normally used by Head Start), and teach some parents the play therapy skills to help them better interact with their children about feelings (Guerney 2014; Ortwein 1997).

These opportunities for the children and parents in Head Start were of great assistance to those parents motivated to benefit from these opportunities and for children to benefit from the educational and social development that comes with a well-defined preschool program. As stated earlier, however, this is a good step for a small group of people, but there is so much more in terms of programming and money to assist those who have few opportunities otherwise.

Some of the political problems were apparent during the early 1980s when I worked there. We had a period of excitement that was felt by all those in the preschool community. There were open hearings from the Pennsylvania State Legislature, and one of the congressional leaders had an interest in fully funded and required preschool programming for children with disabilities. We went as a group representing Head Start and the other preschool programs that served the disabled to a meeting with the congressman. Our input was accepted, but the political process slowed this down to a crawl, and it took several years longer in Pennsylvania before mandatory preschool education for those with disabilities was funded.

Another grave issue was the lack of understanding of the parents who lived very poorly but supported the Reagan administration due to the emphasis on family values. Many of the people we encountered had strong religious beliefs and faith, yet on a more practical level dealing with nutrition alone, one of the laughable initiatives of the Reagan administration was that funding for those who did not have good nutrition (i.e., free breakfast and lunch programs) worked with the administrative designation that ketchup be considered a vegetable.

Again, although the Head Start programs offered assistance to children and their families, most of the people involved were women, many of whom were on public assistance, and job programs have always been woefully underfunded. I have many times dealt with the Department of Vocational Rehabilitation, and the people only have limited services available. This will do nothing to change people's lives.

CHAPTER 2

THERE HAVE BEEN EXEMPLARY ROLE models for the more effective management of social issues in this country, for example, Dr. Kenneth B. Clark, who was one of my professors at City College of New York. He was a psychologist of color who was the lead witness in the *Brown v. Board of Education* case in 1954, which led to desegregation laws. He later established a nonprofit organization in Harlem (where City College is located), called Haryou (Harlem Youth Opportunities Unlimited), which focused on funding job programs, daycare programs, and other opportunities in Harlem to give those from the community a fighting chance. Exemplary school programs were established in the Chicago area, as a second example, treating youngsters with respect and exposing them to larger vocabularies and Shakespeare, assuming the best could be brought out in these students.

Ms. Marva Collins was an educator and substitute teacher in the Chicago Public Schools for fourteen years. In her obituary in the *New York Times* (Roberts 2015), he stated that Ms. Collins had opened her own school called Westside Preparatory Academy, where she focused on "phonics, the Socratic Method and the classics and, she insisted, never expected her students to fail" (p. 2).

The emphasis by the government, however, has often been on bringing up test scores, which does little to motivate students. During the Bush administration in the early part of this millennium, No Child Left Behind was enacted. This was to measure students and teachers on the basis of test scores and create requirements to graduate (minimum reading and math scores) and make decisions about teacher employment based on student test scores. My own experience included situations like the following (which, although fictional, is possible based on experiences I have had): A school district in an urban area refused to pay for an out-of-district placement for a young boy who needed this type of learning situation. The argument was that due to No Child Left Behind, they were preserving the boy's rights by placing him in a classroom in the mainstream, although upon observing the class and based on test scores of this young boy, meeting him, and observing him in a classroom setting, it would be clearly impossible for him to comprehend the material. Although the school district would almost always settle if the family had the funds to pay for an effective legal defense, there had been numerous occasions where people would tell me that due to inclusion, which is a process of keeping children in the mainstream (regular classes), special education services could not be provided and therefore refused to classify. These are all obnoxious arguments to not pay additional funds for special education services either in or outside of the school district. In urban areas especially, there is a tendency to act more recklessly in this regard, expecting that the families would not mount a good legal defense because of the cost. Although this may not always happen, the school districts usually determine that it is worth the risk to them because it will happen more times than not, and it is still less expensive in the long run to resist classification, because the few times they are challenged, it is more cost-effective to use this strategy.

The sad thing about this is, the very state and federal government, who is not fully funding the school districts for these services, will then "slap them on the wrist during a legal action" rather than shoulder any of the responsibility that state and federal funding patterns, which are part of the problem, are not what in fact happens, as the state is set up to "protect" the students from these types of abuses by the local school district.

This is why the argument throughout this book will be about state and federal politics and financial constraints leading to disastrous consequences. Funds need to be provided in a way that these problems can be effectively worked through without having to answer to the government but instead must answer to the public, who needs to be satisfied that the problems are being effectively handled due to the logic of the argument rather than the politics of the situation.

CHAPTER 3

I WOULD LIKE TO USE this chapter to talk about some of the more impressive things that I have seen in my career. Some of it is related to excellent funding, and some are related to committed families creating an excellent outcome.

IN 1975, THEN PRESIDENT GERALD Ford signed into law Public Law 94-142, the Education for All Handicapped Children Act of 1975. This led to due process so that parents had to be informed and give consent to the placement of their children in special education.

Before this law, public schools had the right to place children in any classes they wanted to. In other words, if a student had trouble with learning, they could test children without consulting with parents and place children in any special education classes they wanted. This led to some absolutely horrendous situations. The atmosphere created in the public schools led to the expression "tard class." This was the class for students who were referred to as mentally retarded. They were made fun of, treated with complete lack of respect, and outright tortured on some occasions. There are many stories in high schools of gang rape, where a group of boys had taken sexual liberties with a young girl who was mentally retarded and just looking for affection. This is a sad state of affairs that the people in this country can express such abject cruelty, but it has happened many times.

Parents who had enough of this type of treatment toward their children banded together to form the Association for Retarded Citizens (ARC). This has led to many more educational opportunities, sheltered workshops so that young adults would have a workplace when they were of age, and small group homes where these young men and women could live and have a lifestyle that they could be proud of. It also led to many more classes, some funded by ARC, for students in need of an education. It was often true that the more severely mentally retarded students were deemed uneducable and not entitled to an education. These individuals were systematically excluded from the schools and remained at home. Parents often had no recourse in those days with no support but to place their children in institutional settings. The first outcry that I can remember was initiated in New York by a then young reporter named Geraldo Rivera. He began an investigative report of an institution of this nature in Staten Island New York—Willowbrook. The deplorable condition of this institution has been well documented. An educational reform movement was taking root. I will talk more specifically about how the Education for All Handicapped Children Law (PL-12-94-142) came into effect later in the book, which led to due process for parents and the beginnings of specialized education plans (IEPs), which required parent permission to implement as the document by which special education services would be administered.

The law, although enacted in 1975, was first enforced on October 1, 1977. There would be a meeting with parents to decide whether the student should receive special education services. If the multidisciplinary team (in Pennsylvania) or Child Study Team (in New Jersey) decided a child was eligible for special education services, the team would develop an IEP, or individualized education plan, along with the special education teacher who would be teaching the student. This would include all the goals and objectives for learning in the various areas of the curriculum. The beauty of an IEP is that the child with this document is not measured against the other students but against his or her own progress. It gives the child a chance to learn at his or her own pace. If the child is able to enter the mainstream at some point, the child will then feel more accomplished, and often the learning experience allows the child to "catch up." If not, there are vocational tracts that happen later to allow a child to work in meaningful ways. This too is fraught with many obstacles, as the child who needs vocational training is often at the end of their educational career connected with the Division of Vocational Rehabilitation. As again is true of many state and federal agencies, they fall short in their ability to train and place individuals into meaningful jobs. Because of ARC, there are many more opportunities for cognitively impaired students because these devoted parents have made sure that this can happen.

Again, with the right planning and management, there can be successful outcomes. I had the good fortune to be thrown into the midst of the beginning stages of 94-142, and I feel grateful to have been there at the very start. The reason for this is that I began my doctoral career at Penn State in September 1977, and as I said earlier, 94-142 was enforced beginning on October 1, 1977.

When I first came to Penn State, I did not know how I would support myself. I found out within a couple of days that I would receive a graduate assistantship, which paid my tuition and a small stipend for living expenses. I would be working as a school psychologist on a federal grant through the Department of Speech and Language Services. The grant was called the Multiply Handicapped Hearing Impaired Project (MHEP), which funded me to work at two state schools in central Pennsylvania. State schools were institutions for the mentally retarded. In addition to the living arrangements for these individuals, there was a school program that was connected not only to the state school but also to the local intermediate unit, which was a state agency charged in counties in Pennsylvania with the responsibility of providing services too expensive for the individual districts to provide.

I worked under the supervision of the school psychologist at the primary location, and there was a demonstration project at one of the classes. Nobody at that time had a real idea about what IEPs were to look like, as the first ones were to be prepared by October 1, 1977, and I began with this grant in September. We all learned together. There were many dedicated people teaching these students. I tested all the students and tried to develop behavior management programs where necessary for the students in this classroom. I was exposed to a range of students, but many were moderately to severely cognitively impaired in addition to being hearing impaired. These students would most probably spend the rest of their lives in specialized settings, but when the disabilities were less severe, there were also opportunities (say, with students who had a more mild learning disability) to become increasingly more involved in general education once they had caught up and compensated for their disability.

As PL 94-142 was never fully funded, I have seen many failures in placing students in the right classes to meet their needs and in mainstreaming (placing disabled students in general education for either part or all their education when the students were ready), where people do not take the time and effort to do this properly. Without adequate preparation, these attempts at mainstreaming can often blow up. There are wealthier districts who do this much more effectively, and again we come back to the issues on poverty and inner-city or rural and underfunded schools.

Fast-forward to my recent experiences, as there was a period when I worked as a psychologist for a company providing services to ARC. Services to ARC are often provided in the form of sheltered workshops for cognitively impaired youngsters who are able to work and day programs for the more severely and profoundly cognitively impaired. The company I worked for provided speech services, OT services, and psychotherapy. I of course was involved in psychotherapy, setting up behavioral programs, etc.

At the workshop, it was amazing to watch the enthusiasm of these mostly young men and women who clocked in to work every day, had a work station, received paychecks, and had a lunch hour. At the end of a long work week (this workshop was in an inner-city setting), it would be time to dance to the "Macarena." The song would be played, and there would be dancing, singing, and true joy. I am not at all opposed to mainstreaming when it is done properly, but there is a great deal to be said for being with your peers and feeling comfortable, secure, and good about yourself because the work is something you can do, you are supported for your accomplishments, and you are with your peers.

Likewise, although the limiting side again goes back to what the state provides, are group home living arrangements. Each state's Department of Developmental Disabilities (DDD) has long waiting lists for placement into the limited number of group homes available. It can sometimes take up to six or seven years to be placed in a living arrangement. However, once placed, the young men and women have a living situation with some level of supervision. They get to go to the mall and spend their earnings as they choose, decorate their room as they choose, and live a lifestyle that allows an experience of self-respect.

At another point in my career, I worked as a psychologist for a special school program for the moderately to severely neurologically impaired. This means that their learning disability is severe enough that they would fare better in a special school setting than in their own district. The beauty of this school program is that is has been very well funded. They had a charity run and a fashion show that brought in excellent funding for the school.

One of the amazing things about this school is that in addition to their stellar educational program, they began as early as age six with prevocational activities that led to vocational activities for all the students. For those students who could work in the community, they had an effective job coaching program, and it led to the jobs talked about above as well as to their sheltered workshop for those students who needed this type of environment. This was one of the few special education schools that I am aware of that was designated a Blue Ribbon School by the federal government. At this school there was once a musical show attended by parents. I remember distinctly a teenage girl who attended the school, and because of her disability, she could not remember the words to any song she might sing. The speech department set her up so she could lip sync to the song, and with this in place, she had the mannerisms of a rock star, which created great happiness for this young lady and her parents.

This is my objection to mainstreaming. If done properly, mainstreaming can be a great ego boost to the student who has caught up to his or her peers and is able to participate with other students who do not have a disability. However, when done poorly and with a lack of planning, the student is sometimes left to flounder.

At another time in my career, I worked for a sheltered workshop for cognitively impaired adults. I had discussed this as it pertained to their workshop ritual involving singing and dancing to the "Macarena" at the end of a work week. The workshop also placed people in outside employment. Although the workshop placed many procedural safeguards in place, it would be possible for a student to be placed in a corporation (i.e., fast-food place, toy store, etc.).

The corporation takes care of scheduling and placement, and things may conceivably happen that were unintended because the corporation does not set things up well. For example, an employee who is not from the workshop can conceivably start a commotion by baiting or making fun of the employee from the workshop, a young woman can be placed in a compromising position because her naïveté does not adequately provide protection for the individual, or an individual is fired by a supervisor who might even be younger than the employee because they are not sensitive to the needs of that individual. Although safeguards are put in place, it is no guarantee that these things cannot happen as these workplaces are putting forth an effort to hire the impaired so that they are not being discriminatory, but they are not putting in place all the safeguards that are necessary to ensure the safety and well-being of the workers who have been placed there from the sheltered workshop.

CHAPTER 4

THE CLEAREST DIFFERENCE IS THAT services for those with limited resources are available through some variation of Medicaid reimbursement. The most limited pay to professionals for services is through Medicaid. Although this program started in 1965 at the same time Medicare allowed for some level of medical services for those with limited resources, it is often true that many of the most well-trained and experienced providers of service do not accept Medicaid patients.

However, the insurance community, either in the private or in the public sector, is equating things that do not equate in order to save money. There are three degree tracks that result in the ability to provide independent counseling services to the public: doctoral level psychologist, licensed clinical social worker, and licensed professional counselor. Although psychologists are paid a little more money, it is not substantial enough a difference to draw psychologists into the field, and this is designed to drive down the cost of service. It is also reinforcing social workers and professional counselors for their own interests to present themselves as being equal to psychologists. If LCSWs and LPCs are master's level degree tracks and getting the license is less rigorous, how can you compare these professionals as equal to psychologists, who go on for their doctorate and have a more rigorous training track to obtain a professional license?

I will be presenting case studies and interviews during the course of this book that are reprinted with permission of the family.

The first is about an impressive woman of color who did not grow up in the inner city. This is a significant factor, as the upbringing here is paramount in this story, and the successful outcome with her two boys, which I have observed and experienced, is directly related to a level of motivation to succeed, which is often obliterated when growing up in the inner city.

The woman I am referring to has a good job for a large company. She had decided in raising her two adopted sons that it would make the most sense to have a home that she could afford. She therefore bought an older but nice home in the inner city in an area that was relatively safe, and they had set up a nice life there.

The point here is that she did not grow up in the inner city. I have no doubt that she has experienced her fair share of racism, but it is the mind-set that I am most concerned about in writing this book. She therefore would have been educated and grown up in a wealthier Community, which is far from growing up with the self-defeating mind-set, which I have experienced from individuals who have grown up in the inner city.

This single parent had decided to become a foster parent through Child Protective Services and went through their training. Her home was approved as a foster home, and she ultimately received one of the two brothers we talked about at birth and, ultimately, the second of the two brothers. They were removed from a family involved with Child Protective Services, and when the rights of the parents were terminated, she filed for and was approved to adopt both boys. The three now constitute a happy and thriving nuclear family.

At the time of the adoption, she did not know what ultimately became clear, that both boys have been diagnosed with autism. The basic understanding we have of this diagnosis does not relate as was originally thought to non-nurturing parents, but in fact is more related to genetic factors that have to do with the development of language skills. Although those with severe autism may have no language or rather limited language skills, there are many like her two sons who are very verbal and, in the case of her boys, quite hyperactive. One of the areas that are clearly identified with autism is the lack of ability to read social cues or understand social situations. It often appears to people with this diagnosis that they are clueless about how people work or how relationships work. One group that falls under this diagnosis are people with high-functioning autism or Asperger's disorder.

Some people with autism or Asperger's disorder are very bright cognitively. An image that is well done and people can relate to, which demonstrates people who view the world in this fashion, is the TV show *The Big Bang Theory*.

The two brothers I am talking about are very different in this way. The oldest has more issues cognitively and needs special classes not only related to his autism but also related to his learning. The younger brother, however, is very bright, although he is substantially more hyperactive. What struck me when I began seeing the two when the eldest was about age six and the youngest was about age four is that the youngest astounded us by correctly using the word *fedora* (a hat) when he was about four years of age.

The elder brother has some real talent artistically, and his younger brother is more the athlete. As I hope this is making clear, I see these two brothers as others who know them do as individuals with distinct personalities, not as autistic brothers. The label is only there to advocate for this group and to identify the types of services they might need—period!

As their mom began to find out what they needed, she has been by far their strongest advocate, and she will fight fiercely for what they need. She was even able to negotiate with the city to install a handicapped parking spot in front of their home.

As the boys were at that time ages six and four, the best therapeutic mode was play therapy. This involves teaching the mom to do play therapy sessions and learn the skills that help them develop language that will better express their feelings. The parent observes their play and labels the feelings, giving them the opportunity to hear what the feelings are called and then to learn to verbalize the feelings over time.

At first, their mom was very skeptical, but over time, she began to see a difference in her own behavior (as it is often frustrating to deal with the hyperactivity and lack of understanding of two boys with autism and hyperactivity) and also their behaviors related to describing their own feelings. It was more, however, than offering them play therapy. These boys needed to have exposure to their environment to begin to understand it. Over time, we got her eldest son involved in art classes and her youngest son in sports. Her eldest son did not want to be left out, and he too participated to some degree in sports.

Another key issue relates to their education. As stated earlier, inner-city schools make limited resources available in special education because of its size. I was involved with her in the early stages of fighting for the boys to be in a specialized school environment, which would be out of district. The district balked at it and would not cooperate. However, she had tremendous survival skills, patience, and persistence, and she gradually worked through the politics in an amazing way and prevailed, having them placed in specialized classes in a local Special Education School District. Although the kids are no longer in this program but in another special school, she has been so amazing that she is currently on the board of this Special Education School District. The boys are doing well, and I am still in touch with the family. There are many different ways to accomplish things and different approaches can work one family at a time, but to make the system work better, it will take a great deal of money. Based on my experiences, it is hard to imagine dramatic changes without tapping into private monies, which I will address more fully toward the end of this book.

PART II

A Historical Perspective

CHAPTER 5

I CAME TO THE CITY College of the City University of New York at a very exciting time. I got there in September 1970. This was at the tail end of protesting against the Vietnam War. The Students for a Democratic Society (SDS) had taken over several college campuses to protest the war—most notably, Berkley in California and Columbia University, which was just down the road from us in New York City. The antiwar movements in some of the larger cities such as New York left college campuses and made its way into the high schools. Having spoken with many other people over the years who did not grow up in a major city, they were not affected by the antiwar movement to the same extent that I was growing up in New York.

It became intimidating in some ways, however, because there was an aggressive side to this form of protest. Most of us were protesting for peace, but there were angry people at that time, and we marched up Sixth Avenue from Church and Murray Streets, which was the then location of the IRS building, to Bryant Park at Forty-Second Street near the public library. It was at Bryant Park that there were folk singers, such as Pete Seeger, and the crowd was riled up by all the excitement. While we marched, police were on the left side of us to keep the peace and not only to ensure that the march was peaceful but also to ensure that none of us were hit by bottles or other debris coming from the buildings above us. Although the march was peaceful, it had this intimidating edge.

Here is the issue and how it relates to the contents of this book. The boundaries at this time were often blurred. It was a group of teenagers who were becoming so powerful in their message that it caused Lyndon Baines Johnson to drop out of the race for presidency in 1968 because blame was cast upon him and brought to the forefront by these protests for his continued bombing of South Vietnam and the surrounding areas.

Lyndon Johnson had also become involved with the largest-scale domestic political agenda since the New Deal was initiated by President Franklin Delano Roosevelt because he could manipulate his way through Congress with greater ease than most. Johnson therefore initiated the War on Poverty, and this led to the beginnings of Medicare and Medicaid, which were federal programs offering medical services paid for by the government to the senior citizens and those who fell below the poverty guidelines.

Although much of this information has been written about before, it is important to keep in mind the blurring of boundaries as the protests against the war and the militant protests for the rights of people of color began to merge into one large attack on the government and its power to control the money going to individuals in the United States. The large cry was attacking the Military Industrial Complex where large sums of money were diverted to keep a strong military, and money was not going to meet the domestic needs at home with the same level of interest. The disenfranchised were becoming a louder voice, and in 1967, there were large and violent protests in large cities around the United States, including the Watts section of Los Angeles and Newark, New Jersey.

The message of peace sought after by bombing military installations or the shooting of four students at Kent State University in Ohio makes no sense. How can you take a warlike approach to seek peace? Yet groups of black militants and college students joined forces to try to intimidate the government, and it is pretty hard to scare people who have guns and other weapons. The students lost their luster and went underground, and the black militants became a group of unhappy and disenfranchised individuals whom, after a period of time, people stopped listening to. In my opinion, it was the message of Martin Luther King Jr., who stressed nonviolence, that had a more lasting effect on the public consciousness.

The question becomes, how do you get money to the right people who need it the most? I am not opposed to a strong military, but one that safeguards the United States without ignoring its people. The people who live in the United States have a right to a sense of well-being right here at home. It is clear that the streets in the inner city are not safe; there is a rampant drug trade, and many people live in fractured families who are receiving a poor education. It is these problems that I have become concerned with. I do believe that private funding can be utilized to assist in solving these problems far more than is the case currently.

CHAPTER 6

ONE OF MY PROFESSORS AT City College of New York was Dr. Kenneth B. Clark. He had become famous as he was a man of color who was raised in Harlem, which was the location of City College. In 1954, the legal case *Brown v. Board of Education of Topeka, Kansas,* led to the ruling that schools should no longer be segregated.

In a blog issued by Harvard University Press on July 17, 2014, a piece was published entitled "The Unknown Kenneth B. Clark." It was published in part to commemorate the fiftieth anniversary of the Civil Rights Act, which was signed into law in 1964 by Lyndon Johnson. The article was written by Daniel Matlin to whom I am grateful for his permission to use, with proper citations large, sections of the blog to help this book come alive. The article went on to report that "the summer of 1964 also witnessed the Harlem Riot, an event that inaugurated years of urban uprisings which broke any illusion that America's racial divisions had been laid to rest. It was 60 years ago that the Supreme Courts' ruling in Brown v. Board of Education shattered the legal foundations underpinning segregation" (*Matlin,* 2014 p. 1).

The blog went on to point to Kenneth B. Clark's vital contribution in coordinating the expert witness testimony cited in the Brown ruling. "Segregated schools, the Court was persuaded, stigmatized and harmed black children by their very nature, regardless of whether white and black schools were equally resourced. The famous 'doll tests' through which Clark and his wife, Mamie Phipps Clark—like him, a psychologist trained at Howard and Columbia Universities— had exposed black children's marked preference for white dolls still provides perhaps the most graphic and abiding image of the interior, emotional costs of institutionalized white supremacy" (*Matlin*, 2014 p. 1).

I would have no doubt that in 1954, there was great fear modeled in black homes about expressing preferences for black dolls. Not to mention the fact that it was years before that toy companies tried to produce black dolls, which were nowhere to be seen, I am sure, in 1954. Also, how would this relate to Native Americans, people from Latin America, or people who are cognitively impaired?

My point is that there are many disenfranchised groups, and integration alone does not serve to solve much deeper and far-reaching problems. I would agree, however, that better financed schools create better learning opportunities.

These are the dangers of politicizing the issues, where everyone has their own agenda and political interpretation of the truth determines the best course of action. What I am advocating is that the best trained people need to lead the way, and money needs to be channeled to these individuals, whether it is psychologists, drug rehab specialists, or specialists in job coaching, so that the individuals who need to be better prepared and better motivated are in a position to receive the help that they need by the most competent people. This would also apply to individuals working in the schools, which would include teachers, administrators, and staff who diagnose and place children in special education programs.

Private funding needs to be obtained, which either is used to set up independent programs or works to supplement government money to fund entities that can do the job properly.

Two issues come up at this point, which are the issue of underfunding and, secondly, the issue of politicizing the process. In an article from the *New York Times* dated August 26, 1964, by Sydney H. Schanberg, the headline reads, "HARYOU WILL GET" (Schanberg 1964). Haryou stands for Harlem Youth Opportunities Unlimited. It was an organization started in Harlem by Dr. Kenneth B. Clark to improve the lot of Harlem's seventy-one thousand youths.

The article goes on to say that "Dr. Arthur Logan, chairman of the board of Haryou-Act, disclosed that the agency would probably sign contracts with the city and Federal governments for $4.4 million by the end of the week or early next week. Up to now, the Harlem antipoverty and youth program calls for spending $118 million over a three-year period, only about $450,000 had been received. That came from the city and was earmarked for research and planning" (Schanberg 1964, p. 1).

Do the math on this! Their operating budget then would be $5 million compared with the $118 million that was planned for over a three-year period. This is a shortage of $113 million. Haryou-Act was created from two community action groups. Haryou was the brainchild of Dr. Kenneth B. Clark, and ACT was a community action group initiated by the then US Congressman for Harlem—Adam Clayton Powell. According to the article, "the ACT funds were distributed as follows: adult volunteer service corps, $255,229; after-school study program, $4,410,627; domestic peace corps, $1,277,328; day-care residential treatment for disturbed children, $3,037,643; and central administration, $1,694,059. The rest of the budget was appointed as follows: training of workers, $2,778,505; five local neighborhood boards, $2,587,695; Harlem Youth Unlimited, $5,003,635; pre-school academies, $26,752,615; after-school study centers, $3,423,987; employment centers, $25,470,631; services to multi-problem families, $1,443,324; junior academies, $8.706,950; senior academies, $4,583,000; narcotics research center, $4,967,745; cadet corps, $7,605,750; arts and cultural affairs, $5,969,658; research, $928,949; and central administration, $7,178,355" (Schanberg 1964, p. 3).

The article goes on to state that "little of the money, which is expected from Federal, state, city and foundation sources, has as yet been allocated. Mayor Wagner announced that the city would budget $3.4 million for Haryou-Act in 1964–65, and the President's Committee on Juvenile Delinquency has promised $1 million" (Schanberg 1964, p. 3).

It can be seen based on the budgetary figures that only a very small percentage, approximately 1 percent of the funding, was allocated for general research. Although $5 million was allocated for narcotics research, this is still a fairly small percentage of the entire budget. The approach with Haryou was based on anticipated funding from the federal government. Community Action Programs were set up to "wage the war on poverty," which called for community boards to express what the community needed, and one of these services was Head Start. The largest budget item for Haryou was for preschool programs. The second-largest budget line was for employment centers. It did make sense that the program demanding the largest budget line made decisions about its own funding (as stated earlier, this was one of the issues that impeded the growth of Head Start Programs as the Community Action Programs controlled the budget even though the biggest line item was Head Start).

A further problem here is that at the time that Public Assistance Rolls swelled, there was a large and negative sentiment at the federal level against the government providing financial support for families. The belief, and rightly so, was that the families would become dependent on this government support. However, the second-biggest budget line was for employment centers. The truth be told, jobs were becoming more available outside of the inner city, and men who could work were in fact leaving their families to take these jobs as the welfare rolls consisted largely of widows and orphans. An intact family with two parents could not collect public assistance at that time. It was forcing men to leave their families and seek employment elsewhere, and further, the interstates had made it easier to leave the city and seek jobs in the suburban areas around the city. This began to give rise to the black middle class as those families who could leave did, and the single-parent families where the father left and his family was not in a position to follow stayed behind. Many of those who were left behind, both men and women, could not find jobs. Job training might have been available to a small percentage of people and might have worked for some. However, if you look at state services through the Department of Vocational Rehabilitation, they were not effective in providing many meaningful job opportunities, especially as the US economy worsened. There were people who had criminal records, people still on drugs or in rehab programs, and as public assistance did become available as well to men and their families, people who relied on the state to pay for housing and benefits.

The other factor that is critical here is the belief in the local neighborhood boards. The goal was that input from the people who lived in the community would identify the needs of the community. Not meaning to be insulting but more logical, this is like giving the keys for the car to someone who never learned to drive. Without training, how could the people in the inner city identify solutions to these problems? I would agree that their input is critical to identifying the problem areas, but you need trained people to offer empirically based procedures that have been well researched to actually solve these problems. This is not a put-down, but when you give people this level of control and do not train them properly, human nature is such that the local boards would try to assert their power without proper guidance. As this is doomed to fail, the politicians will then swoop in and take over for "the misguided people who could not manage their own neighborhoods." Instead, more money needs to be spent on training, and as can be seen from the figures, the training of workers is budgeted at half the level than the budget for research!

What ultimately did happen in many cases was that the politicians did take over, and the boards were unsuccessful in managing their community, their schools, etc., and the feelings of failure and loss of self- esteem grew even higher. This conflict continues today with few results that can be documented. For example, the Philadelphia Public Schools, close to bankruptcy, were taken over by a private corporation; the prisons as well have been privatized, but these may turn out to be financially effective but not necessarily yielding a better product. Schools have been closed in Philadelphia, for example, and the costs may go down; but to the best of my knowledge, there has been no demonstration of a better education for its students. This has led to alternative, charter schools, which are again run from within the community and provide an alternative education but are often underfunded and do not necessarily, for this reason alone, provide a better education. Although as stated earlier, there are unique individuals like Marva Collins; they are few and far between.

The *New York Times* article by Mr. Schanberg went on to state that in June 1964, a bitter leadership controversy erupted in the days preceding the merger of Harlem Youth Activities Unlimited

(Haryou) and Associated Community Teams, which was sponsored by Mr. Adam Clayton Powell (Schanberg 1964). This reached all the way up to the federal level as Mr. Powell was on the committee in Congress, which approved funding for these programs.

The article included a warning from Dr. Clark. The article stated that "Dr. Kenneth B. Clark, the City College psychologist considered the father of Haryou, accused Representative Adam Clayton Powell, the sponsor of ACT, of trying to handpick the executive director to control the Haryou-Act program for his political purposes. In late July, 1964, Dr. Clark resigned from the Haryou-Act board with a warning that the agency's antipoverty program was doomed if it were used to 'perpetuate political dynasties'" (Schanberg, pp. 2–3).

An article was written in the *New York Times* on June 25, 1965, by Paul L. Montgomery. It was entitled "Haryou-Act Sets $118 Million Budget" (Montgomery 1965). The article stated that Haryou and ACT would merge, and the combined program set a three-year budget of $118 million. Lyndon Johnson at that time wanted an ambitious agenda regarding antipoverty and civil rights, and this was said to be his follow-through on the ambitious agenda that would have been John F. Kennedy's legacy had he lived. This was about the time in Johnson's career where he had taken over as president and at first wanted to be perceived as carrying through on the Kennedy agenda (as he had yet to be elected president, which happened in November of that year), and also in November of that year, Bobby Kennedy was elected senator from New York.

Politically, Sargent Shriver, who was a brother-in-law to the Kennedys, was appointed head of the antipoverty programs, including the Peace Corps and Head Start. The Kennedys were therefore intimately involved in this agenda, and as will be seen later, when asked by Dr. Clark for some backing in New York, he declined to help him as he did not want to alienate one of the people in Congress as he was running for president at that time (1967) and, as a result, implicitly threw his support behind Representative Powell.

The article went on to state that Dr. Clark had been involved for three weeks in a controversy with Representative Adam Clayton Powell, as each had accused the other of trying to take over the program. One of the charges made by Mr. Powell's supporters was that almost 10 percent of the three-year budget for Haryou-Act was to go to the Northside Center for Child Development, 31 West 110th Street, which was run by Dr. Clark and his wife, Dr. Mamie Phipps Clark.

The budget report by the Haryou board noted that the only fund earmarked for helping psychologically disturbed children was about $8 million to be spent by ACT (Mr. Powell's program) for two residential treatment day-care centers.

The article went on to state that Dr. Clark had acknowledged that he would withhold further criticism of Mr. Powell to ease the task of the combined board and they would meet again shortly. However, a former public relations man for Mr. Powell declared that a "Harlem citizens committee" would bring suit in federal court to restrain the government from releasing federal funds to Haryou-Act as it is now constituted.

The goal was to force the dissolving of the present board, as the "All-Harlem Leadership Committee" formed from among Mr. Powell's supporters was taking court action because the board was not considered representative of the Harlem community.

John H. Young, the coordinator of this committee, contended that the current constitution of the board could lead to a takeover by the city of New York and by groups more interested in themselves than they were in the great majority of Negro people of Harlem.

In my own experiences working in the inner city, there was great mistrust in me as a trained professional as someone who might be trying to hurt the families I was hired to serve. In fact, this was the last thing I intended, and although many of the families would prefer to speak to someone of their own culture (predominately black or Hispanic), there were few trained psychologists who were from these ethnic groups, and my training and experience were devalued as something that could be of assistance. It is not patronizing of me to state that training and experience are needed to help resolve family problems, and there is no question that others from the same culture may better understand some of the needs so long as they are well trained. Part of what contributes to this resistance is repeated experiences with Child Protective Services, which is out to monitor and not assist the people they are responsible for. By the same token, the tensions with the local police persist because of bad experiences with the police, and these opinions of mistrust are not often swayed if the police officer just happens to be black or Hispanic. The mere fact that they are working for the police department is enough reason to mistrust.

CHAPTER 7

AN ARTICLE WAS RUN BY the *Atlantic Monthly* written by Nicholas Lemann entitled "The Unfinished War" (Lemann 1988). The article reported the following quote from Ronald Reagan during his presidency: "In the sixties we waged a war on poverty, and poverty won." The article went on to state, "There is a widespread perception that the federal government's efforts to help the poor during the sixties was almost unlimited; that despite them poverty became more severe, not less; and that the reason poverty increased is that all those government programs backfired and left their intended beneficiaries worse off."

The article went on to say that "the truth is that the percentage of poor Americans went down substantially in the sixties. The idea that poverty increased comes from what people know about conditions in inner-city black ghettos, where unemployment, crime, illegitimacy, drug abuse, and physical decay did worsen through most of the sixties and afterward, even while the rate of black poverty overall was dropping. There is a strong temptation to see the ghettos as the embodiment of some king of fundamental rottenness at the core of social welfare liberalism."

One of the problems, however, as relayed in the article was that "almost no effort was made to find out what kinds of anti-poverty programs already worked and then to expand them" (p. 2).

"The War on Poverty looked for solutions to poverty that would be local and diffuse and would circumvent state and local government and Congress" (p. 2). Hate developed from the politicians, and the War on Poverty was in trouble politically from its start. "Its planners hoped to build public support for it by achieving quick, visible successes, but in setting up hundreds of separate anti-poverty organizations run largely by inexperienced people, this practically guaranteed that there would be quite a few highly publicized failures. These turned public opinion against the War on Poverty" (p. 2).

Although the goal of these antipoverty programs was to revive the ghettos as communities, the ghettos were dying because millions of their residents were moving out into new and better off black neighborhoods. Although the focus of this article is on the black community, the same facts are in evidence for Hispanics and other disenfranchised groups. They left the ghetto often to fill leadership positions in local government or state government. The community action programs helped create leaders, and these leaders then left the communities often for something better.

One of the arguments of the 1960s was that you could not relate to people in the ghetto unless you lived there. This resulted in some people choosing to stay even though they had the money to leave. However, these individuals could leave whenever they wanted, and this is a huge difference. It is also true that such leaders as Dr. Kenneth B. Clark lived in Westchester County even though originally raised in Harlem. Does this mean you cannot help if you choose not to live in poverty? My experience is that in social agencies, such as Child Protective Services, there is a strong effort to hire people who can relate to the population in ghetto communities, so Latin Americans who speak Spanish will more easily relate to the families for whom they are the caseworker, and black caseworkers can relate better to black families. However, where this breaks down is the fact that I was often asked to work with Hispanic families where I did not speak the language, even with an interpreter present, because there are so few Hispanic psychologists. There certainly are Hispanic psychologists and psychiatrists, but too few to cover the largesse of the population in the inner city.

There are other such boundary issues that come up. What if you are from Chile and have a different accent or dialect than a family from the Dominican Republic, or what if you are from Africa and your accent is hard to understand for blacks who were born in New Jersey? This is not to say there are not elegant and intelligent clients from Africa or caseworkers from Africa who have an excellent command of the language, but this is far from always the truth. This ethnic matching process is far from perfect. An example that sticks in my mind involved my work for an education class when I was attending City College. It was a middle school, and families would migrate from their home countries in Latin America to the United States and back again, and to create some comfort and decrease tensions, the principal of the middle school tried to set up Dominican areas of the school and Puerto Rican areas of the school and so on. Is this considered segregation, or creating comfort for the children of varied cultures who attended that school? There are many vocal attacks about segregation, blacks who are successful and becoming Uncle Toms, and psychologists who no longer represent the needs of the majority of clients who live in Harlem, because although you were raised there, you do not live there now, as in the case of Dr. Clark. My point is, you need the most experienced leaders to manage the issues and the money, and this cannot be solved by vocal finger-pointing or the need to be politically correct.

CHAPTER 8

ALTHOUGH ROBERT KENNEDY AND LYNDON Johnson were the two biggest advocates who were politicians in the twentieth century to push the agenda to fight poverty, their inability to get along and their mistrust for each other made it impossible for them to fight together. According to Lemann in his article in the *Atlantic Monthly*, accomplishing the goals became untenable unless both were fighting on the same side (Lemann 1988).

Johnson's initial fear after the assassination of President Kennedy was that he would be compared to the former president in an unfavorable way. The liberals who would support antipoverty were not a fan of Johnson. The liberal, intellectual establishment saw him as a "hick from the Southwest." It was JFK's intent to initiate an attack on poverty, and Johnson, once he became president, was in favor of this. Bobby Kennedy, however, framed out this program as JFK's last wish and therefore did not originate with LBJ.

Lemann's article went on to say that beginning after World War II, there was a migration of blacks from the South who settled in the cities to the North, and the majority settled in what were becoming urban ghettos. In my own experience, many of these ethnic neighborhoods had been populated by Jews, Italians, and Irish, and with the GI Bill and the growth of the population, many of these families moved out to the suburbs. Rent-controlled apartments in the urban areas became attractive to blacks moving up from the South, and these areas began to decay with age.

According to Lemann's article, "by the Fall of 1965 Lyndon Johnson's poverty program would stand as the national government's chief direct response to the problems of the northern ghettos to which the migrants came, but the program was conceived with only the haziest understanding of what the ghettos' problems were" (p. 7).

One of the focal points of the problems in the ghetto, which is still a hot topic today, is gang violence. In the early 1960s, however, the term utilized to describe what happened to urban poor teenagers was *juvenile delinquency*. The belief was expressed by Albert Cohen in his book *Delinquent Boys*, published in 1955, which explained delinquency as the result of a realization by lower-class kids that they couldn't have middle-class success and so had to set up an alternative status system in which they could succeed.

In the fall of 1961, David Hackett, Robert Kennedy's best friend from prep school, became the chairman of the Committee on Juvenile Delinquency. In 1960, Cloward and Ohlin published *Delinquency and Opportunity* and argued that delinquents turned to crime not out of a sense of failure but because society had denied them any other path of opportunity (Lemann, 1988 p. 11). "The idea of insufficient opportunity as the cause of delinquency was the guiding principle of the Committee on Juvenile Delinquency as it made grants to organizations all over the country, several of them working in urban black ghettos" (Lemann, 1988 p. 12).

"At the level of practical politics there was (and still is) a fundamental hostility in congressional and public opinion to the idea of an American welfare state, especially one that gives money to poor people. The biggest social-welfare program, Social Security, travels under the guise of an insurance policy; Aid to Families With Dependent Children, the main program for making cash grants to the poor, was created along with Social Security in 1935 and was billed as a kind of pension plan for widows and orphans rather than a welfare system. Even though it has been believed for decades that AFDC encourages the formation of single-parent families, only last September (1987) did Congress pass a provision making all two-parent poor out-of-work families in the country eligible for welfare" (Lemann, 1988 p. 13).

During the Kennedy administration, the belief was that small bureaucracies in the local neighborhoods (Community Action Programs) were far less expensive and far more efficient than creating a large unwieldy bureaucracy at the national level. The community boards could find out the needs of the people in their own community and coordinate existing services to provide for these needs. "How, it now seems fair to ask, could there have been so much faith in the ability of a program INSIDE the ghettos to increase the amount of opportunity available to the people living there?" (Lemann, 1988 p. 17).

"The interstate highway system and urban renewal (or, to use the nickname critics gave it, "Negro removal") were to liberals' minds two of the great mistakes of the Eisenhower years, promoting downtown business development and suburban sprawl at the expense of vibrant, though poor, inner-city communities" (p. 17).

These problems worsened with the concept of gentrification, where upwardly mobile young people who could not afford the rents of downtown city households were attracted to move into projects in the more urban inner-city areas of the city as a cheap alternative, but these "yuppies" often gave nothing back to the communities in which they lived.

After the death of President Kennedy, Johnson was persuaded to the idea of community action. "For $500 million in new funds, which is what he gave...for poverty fighting, a much more visible program could be created through community action than through more traditional means" (Lemann, 1988 p. 18). As you might remember, we had already talked about the proposal for Haryou, which was $118 million for over three years for the Harlem community action program alone; this would be about a $40 million operating budget for one year, or slightly less than 10 percent of the whole budget. Multiply this by the number of communities in need of service and the number of people who needed help, and this budget falls sadly short. The funding of $500 million falls sadly short if $40 million per year was needed for New York City alone. This would fund only 12 1/2 communities if you look at the money allocated. Far more communities needed funding than just what was made available unless there was an organized pilot program with research data being collected and in fact, it was more like a shotgun approach which was random. Although cheaper, this plan was not thought out clearly, as is often the case for government funding of any social services program. "As he approved community action, Johnson also changed it. The advocates of the idea had intended to start small. Heller's staff wanted ten local community-action agencies, five urban and five rural. Hackett thought that even this was too much, and proposed that the initial funding for the War on Poverty be $1 million a year. But Johnson by nature was not interested in small, slowly developing programs, especially when his first major initiative as President was involved. The President on whom he modeled himself was not, after all, Kennedy, but Franklin D. Roosevelt. ... The poverty program was the opening shot in Johnson's New Deal (termed the Great Society). By the end of January, 1964, the plans were for community action to begin in seventy-five cities" (Lemann, 1988 p. 19).

"As Allen Matusow points out in his book The Unraveling of America, there was no proof at that point (and there still is no proof) that any of the local organizations funded by the President's Committee on Juvenile Delinquency had actually reduced delinquency. Hackett himself said a few years later, 'There've been a great many critics of the program, that it was not successful; and that's probably right.' It was just as unclear whether community-action agencies could reduce poverty. Community action was a totally untested idea that Johnson had suddenly transformed into a large undertaking" (p. 19).

Appointment of Sargent Shriver as head of the War on Poverty (as well as of the Peace Corps) was a nod to the Kennedys as he was Eunice Kennedy's husband, and "so it appeared that Johnson was so deeply loyal to the dead President's desire to fight poverty the he would entrust it only to a family member" (Lemann, 1988 p. 20). However, the Kennedys did not see it the same way and Robert Kennedy wanted to be in that position, and Johnson's having picked Shriver was a rejection of Kennedy. (There had been a running feud between these two that began when Robert Kennedy had requested that Johnson not take the position of vice president when he and Kennedy became the party ticket.)

"Shriver's immediate contribution to community action was to expand it, as a way of improving the War on Poverty bill's chance of passing, even while he was limiting its funding. Within a month of Shriver's appointment the plans called for not ten or seventy-five community action agencies but many more; by 1967 there were more than a thousand. (Future poverty warriors should realize the folly of trying to fund a thousand independent local organizations, most of them new and run by inexperienced people)" (Lemann, 1988 p. 24).

"It had always been a part of the community-action creed that the poor should be consulted about their needs, so that they would get the proper government services. This would be a way to avoid what Robert Kennedy called planning programs 'for the poor, not with them.' Boone believed in this, but there were also other reasons for his idea about putting poor people on community-action boards. First, Boone believed that the cause of poverty was political as well as economic: when a community was poor, the reason was that it lacked power as well as money. Therefore, part of the cure for poverty was empowerment—training the residents of a poor neighborhood to organize themselves and learn to get things from the power structure. Maximum feasible participation was a way of turning the community action boards into a power base for the poor" (Lemann, 1988 p. 25).

"Second, Boone saw the course of community action as a struggle between poor people and social workers, whom he regarded with contempt. Unless some preventive action was taken, social workers would appropriate community action agencies and infuse them with 'the social worker mentality,' in which, for example, all juvenile delinquents were regarded as psychologically troubled and in need of professional help in order to become normal members of society. Boone saw maximum feasible participation as a way of hitting social workers where they lived, challenging them for control over the many social work jobs that community action and the rest of the War On Poverty would create" (Lemann, 1988 p. 25).

Politicians felt threatened by the War on Poverty breaking all the rules and putting money directly in the hands of the people in the impoverished communities without going through normal political channels. The mayor of Chicago at that time was Richard Daley. "Daley considered it essential to maintain total control of all politics and government in Chicago. He personally saw to it that a small HEW grant to Martin Luther King, Jr. for a literacy program in the Chicago ghetto was canceled—after it had been publicly announced—because he considered it wrong for the federal government to put money into Chicago without going through him, especially when the recipient was King. To Daley, community action was the political equivalent of original sin. 'You're putting M-O-N-E-Y in the hands of people who are not in my organization,' he told Bill Moyers. 'They'll use it to bring you down.'" (Lemann, 1988 p. 29).

It was also true that programs that were intertwined with politics and run by inexperienced community people were bound to screw up. "Some of them did, indeed screw up. In Harlem, Adam Clayton Powell demanded a piece of the action at HARYOU, a project whose guiding spirit was the black psychologist Kenneth B. Clark; HARYOU became HARYOU-ACT, Clark resigned in protest, and almost from the moment it received its first OEO grant, of $1.2 million, in June of 1965 HARYOU-ACT was under investigation for financial irregularities. Even in Chicago, where Mayor Daley had been able, through Johnson's intercession, to keep the poverty program totally under his control, an internal OEO report circulated in May of 1965 showed that no books were being kept, that a subcontractor was working without a written contract, and that there was a one-to-one ratio of clerical to professional employees" (Lemann, 1988 p. 31–32).

To sum up, large sums of money were allocated to local neighborhood boards to fight poverty. The boards had a fair share of inexperienced people controlling the money, and they did not always know what to do. Also, the politicians felt threatened by people who controlled the money without involving the politicians.

The main result of all this was that things ramped up too quickly, and money was spent with some theories justifying how the money should be spent to fight delinquency and poverty without looking at proven results. The result was a disaster, and I am sure the programs were never fully funded because the amount of money needed was too much; and as 1965 unfolded, the War on Poverty was eclipsed by the war in Vietnam, which drained large amounts of government money to escalate the war.

CHAPTER 9

THE LEMANN ARTICLE PUBLISHED IN the *Atlantic Monthly* was a two-part piece, and the second piece published in January 1989 (one month later) released a follow-up of the later years. This article talked about the fall of the War on Poverty, which ultimately resulted in Reagan's comments I have reported earlier, which stated that we lost the War on Poverty.

"A few weeks after the assassination Kennedy (Bobby) told Arthur Schlesinger, Jr., 'My brother barely had a chance to get started—and there is so much now to be done—for the Negroes and the unemployed and the school kids and everyone else who is not getting a decent break in our society. ... The new fellow doesn't get this. He knows all about politics and nothing about human beings" (Lemann, part 2, 1989 p. 5).

"In the spring of 1966, during the formulation of Johnson's Model Cities program, which was designed to spend billions on the rehabilitation of the ghettos, Kennedy arrived late at a small dinner attended by several administration officials and delivered a tirade against Model Cities. He said, 'It's too little, it's nothing, we have to do twenty times as much,' says one person who was there. Kennedy began to distance himself from the Johnson Administration. He served as a conduit for a 'peace feeler' from the North Vietnamese, participated in hearings on hunger in Mississippi, helped orchestrate hearings on the urban crisis which were critical of the Johnson Administration, and proposed bills to create two million new public-service jobs and so channel government and private investment into rebuilding the housing stock and employment base in the ghettos. Johnson, a devoted believer in the Getting Things Done faith, had no respect for this kind of position-striking; he considered the real purpose of all Kennedy's actions to be the embarrassment of Lyndon Johnson. He opposed Kennedy's jobs bill, his ghetto development bill, and an expansion of the food-stamps program which was proposed after the hunger hearings" (Lemann, part 2, 1989 p. 5).

"It is commonly said that Vietnam drew Johnson's attention away from the War on Poverty and weakened his financial commitment to it. That may be, but if the war in Vietnam had suddenly ended, Johnson would still have disliked the War on Poverty for having turned out to be, to his mind, a stronghold of his enemies" (Lemann, part 2, 1989 p. 5).

"In the final stages of his presidency the idea of large-scale government programs for the ghettos had become so bound up in his mind with liberal opposition to him that Johnson became positively hostile toward them. He was deeply suspicious of the Kerner Commission, which he had appointed after the terrible Newark and Detroit riots of 1967 to determine how future riots could be avoided. Johnson was convinced that there was a conspiracy behind the riots—in fact, Shriver had to reassure him that OEO (Office of Economic Opportunity) employees were not instigating some of the riots. David Ginsburg, the Kerner Commission's executive director and an old friend of Johnson's, says that when Johnson called him in after his appointment, 'he made it very clear that in his view it was simply not possible to have so many outbreaks at the same time without someone orchestrating it.'

"On April 10, 1968, in the aftermath of Martin Luther King's assassination, Joseph Califano sent Johnson a long memo suggesting that he react to the crisis by making an address to a joint session of Congress, adding billions of dollars to anti-poverty programs, and appointing well-known experts to look into a major re-ordering of the government's fiscal priorities. Johnson, who rarely wrote anything down, scrawled angry comments all over the memo" (Lemann, part 2, 1989 p. 7).

The money lessened, Sargent Shriver and his aides found themselves forced to defend the programs already in place—in particular, community action. Both Johnson and Kennedy hated welfare, and the goals shifted more toward jobs programs as a more viable political alternative. Welfare, it was feared, would create further dependency on the government, and job programs were easier to sell politically. However, a jobs program was far more expensive than a guaranteed income, and for this reason, no large-scale jobs program was ever adopted (Lemann, part 2, 1989).

As the programs being offered as part of the War on Poverty were being struck down, other information was disseminated, which was not well received.

"Toward the end of 1964 Moynihan noticed another significant little fact: although the black male unemployment rate was going down, the number of new black welfare cases was going up. Also, the percentage of black babies born out of wedlock was rising. Moynihan, a man with a journalistic love of the scoop, was eager to get this information out quickly. He decided to begin work on a new report, 'The Negro Family: The Case for National Action.' From the Christmas holidays of 1964 to February of 1965 his staff worked on the report full time, meeting with Moynihan to discuss their progress at the end of every day and not even taking weekends off. Drawing on the work of the sociologist E. Franklin Frazier and the historians Stanley Elkins and Frank Tannenbaum, they assumed that American slavery had been so brutal that it had weakened the traditional husband-wife family structure among blacks, and that the welfare system and high unemployment in the ghettos had hurt the black family still more. Now the ghettos were, as the psychologist Kenneth Clark put it in Dark Ghetto, characterized by 'pathology'" (Lemann, part 2, 1989 pp. 12–13).

"The report did not get attention from the one person in the best position to do something about the problem: Lyndon Johnson. He didn't read it. But it got a fantastic amount of attention in Moynihan's own intellectual world, almost all of it negative and much of it bitterly, wildly, unreasoningly hostile. The Moynihan report might be the single most refuted document in American history, a slim pamphlet to whose discrediting book after book has been devoted. There was a mood change among liberals, after the Watts riots, that coincided almost exactly with the publication of the Moynihan report and caught Moynihan by surprise. For a professor he was not averse to a little rough-and-tumble. He had grown up partly in the slums himself, and was raised by a single mother. He knew what the world was like. His best-known work at the time, the chapter on the Irish in Beyond the Melting Pot, was written with an air of jaunty confidence that the time had come to talk about ethnic-group characteristics (like his own group's drinking) in a frank way, and let the devil take the hindmost. Now, he had come up against the black power movement, which did not like it when a white man described black society as being somehow ruined, and also against the white left, which was becoming less sympathetic to the idea that the values of middle-class America—the values that had gotten us into Vietnam—were so noble that poor people ought to embrace them" (Lemann, part 2, 1989 pp. 13–14).

After all this in-fighting, the only strategy left on the table to fight for was the community action program. "As the community-action creed gained adherents, there was a constant struggle, inside the OEO (Office of Economic Opportunity) and in the liberal press, to push local community-action agencies to serve the 'hard-core poor' rather than the 'easy-to-reach poor,' to steer the funding straight to community groups, bypassing elected officials; and to support strategies of political confrontation instead of accommodation. It was in a way inevitable, given the roots of community action in the theory that juvenile delinquents turn to crime only because of a lack of legitimate opportunity, that the OEO would come to the idea of funding youth gangs. The OEO did so in Chicago" (Lemann, part 2, 1989 p. 15).

The Woodlawn Organization, in Chicago, founded by Saul Alinsky in a black neighborhood on the South Side, was by the midsixties a national model for liberals of how a community organization could turn a ghetto around (though by then the Woodlawn neighborhood was already suffering heavy population losses). Two gangs, the Blackstone Rangers and the East Side Disciples, were engaged in violent warfare over the turf of Woodlawn. Inside the community-action world, the feeling was that the gangs were really part of the legitimate leadership structure of the community and could be made into a positive force if provided with opportunity in the form of a federal grant. In 1967 the research and demonstration division of community action, which was more daring than the operations division, gave the Woodlawn Organization $927,000 to run a job-training program that would use the gang structures of the Rangers and the Disciples to teach teenagers the skills they needed to enter the labor force. The grant "'will put the Blackstone Rangers and the East Side Disciples to work,' Shriver wrote Joseph Califano exultantly. 'The City Police will see that armed fighting stops between the Rangers and the Disciples, and that our money is not used 'to arm both sides'" (Lemann, part 2, 1989 pp. 16).

"The grant was made in June. By December, two of the gang members receiving funds had been arrested on murder charges. (The Blackstone Rangers went on to change their name to the El Rukns and to run into legal trouble for such activities as dealing cocaine and contracting with the Libyan government to carry out terrorist activities in the United States.) The Chicago press and the conservatives in Congress having been handed an example of criminal-coddling by Washington liberals more perfect than they could have dreamed of, launching a flotilla of exposes, denunciations, and hearings. Johnson was furious, and the grant was canceled in 1968—but it is a testament to the power of the idea of community action that many of the people who were leaders of the OEO at the time are still proud of it" (Lemann, part 2, 1989 pp. 16–17).

Employing blacks and others (Hispanics predominately) to run social programs in the inner-city communities was helpful in the beginning of a middle class for those individuals. The greatest successes of community action and community development were to train leaders. "The government social welfare-programs of the sixties—compensatory education Medicare and Medicaid, child nutrition, and so on, as well as programs of the War on Poverty—gave jobs to hundreds of thousands of blacks (many of them the "easy-to-reach" poor the OEO was trying to avoid: that is, people with an education) who used their newfound modest prosperity to leave the ghettos. In effect, all the while that employment programs were losing out to community development programs within the high councils of government, employment was working as a solution to ghetto poverty and community development was not" (Lemann, part 2, 1989 pp. 18–19).

The problem, however, was that these individuals were people who began their education but did not necessarily reach higher levels. They were working within a government system that allowed for a certain job level, and people were also promoted from within, but these social workers and in some cases not even social workers were obtaining jobs in Child Protective Services and other social service areas of the government and were not willing or able to stretch themselves to create a new kind of system. It only served to create a new kind of bureaucrat who needed to preserve their job and not threaten the system even if they saw things that were intuitively wrong. They did not have the knowledge or the power to correct it or rely on those with more knowledge or experience who could find solutions. In Child Protective Services, this wandering band of social workers was basically lost in the woods as they could interface on a culturally appropriate level with the residents they would be assigned to in the local and poor communities but could offer no ideas or hope that the situation that their clients found themselves in would in any way improve.

CHAPTER 10

"Richard Nixon attained the presidency having won probably the smallest percentage of black votes of any President in American history" (Lemann, part 2, 1989 p. 19). "However, if Nixon was shaped by his times, his first term took place in the ideological shadow of the sixties" (Lemann, part 2, 1989). "The programs that followed allowed a great amount of money to be spent on the social services programs whose road map had been laid out by the Johnson Administration. ... However, Nixon's belief system was inconsistent with what was actually being done. Ehrlichman says that on two occasions Nixon told him that he considered blacks to be less intelligent than whites. 'He thought, basically, blacks were genetically inferior,' Ehrlichman says. 'In his heart he was very skeptical about their ability to excel except in rare cases. He didn't feel this way about other groups. He'd say on civil rights things, 'Well, we'll do this, but it isn't going to do any good.' He did use the words 'genetically inferior.' He thought they couldn't achieve on a level with whites" (Lemann, part 2, 1989 pp. 19–20).

During this period, a man by the name of William Shockley emerged. He was an academic from Stanford who was key to the development of the Silicon Valley as the inventor of the transistor. Despite his eminence as a physicist, Shockley publicized his ideas consistent with this Nixon belief system that blacks are genetically inferior. It was about this time in the early 1970s that I attended City College of New York, and my professor whom I had spoken about earlier, Dr. Kenneth B. Clark, the orchestrator of the expert testimony in *Brown v. Board of Education*, was speaking in class about these issues as he had been asked to debate Shockley about the genetic inferiority of blacks. To the best of my knowledge, this debate never happened.

It was about this time at the City College of New York that open enrollment became a reality. It was very hard to get into the city universities because upon admission, tuition would be completely paid by the city of New York (its nickname at City College was the Poor Man's Harvard). If you were poor and had good grades, you could receive a high-quality college education. However, the year before I entered City College, 1969, the campus was locked down by militant blacks who protested a college in their own backyard (Harlem) that they could not attend as they were denied admission unless their grades were high. The argument was that this was racially unfair as the poor education they received in the lower grades would not allow them the opportunity to succeed in school; hence, they deserved a chance to prove what they could do. In comes open enrollment. As of 1970, the year I was admitted to City College (which I had the grades to be admitted anyway), all grade requirements were eliminated, and blacks and Hispanics then had the right to attend the city universities. They needed to take remedial courses to catch up, but hard work at this level would allow them to make up for the poor education they had received before college. This might have helped many, but there were also a fair share of dropouts who could not catch up.

If you stop to think about it, there is nothing more condescending than affirmative action, because it makes the case for genetic inferiority in the sense that it requires a lowering of standards for these disenfranchised groups to succeed. I am not sure that this was the intended outcome of those who fought for affirmative action or for women's rights, etc. You need to favorably compete with your own merits, or it is in fact a hollow victory.

My point throughout this book is that the amount of money spent terribly underfunded these programs, and the people who were hired lacked the experience or power to make a difference. The article goes on to say, "Nixon greatly disliked the programs of the War On Poverty—Head Start, the Jobs Corps, community action—and also Model Cities, the other big Great Society program aimed specifically at the ghettos. 'No increase in any poverty program until more evidence is in,' he wrote Ehrlichman two months after taking office" (Lemann, part 2, 1989 p. 32).

As the Nixon administration moved forward, the strategies moved more toward family assistance or a guaranteed income for the poor. This would eliminate the need to create so many fractured bureaucracies under the federal umbrella and incorporate these strategies into a larger and more uniform effort. "The social workers could hardly complain, because even as the government was cutting them out of the action, it would be passing the most sweeping anti-poverty program in history. They would be neutralized as a moral and political force" (Lemann, part 2, 1989 p. 26).

"Although the Family Assistance Plan (providing a guaranteed annual income to the poor) was never enacted, the record of the first Nixon Administration does look like a victory for the income strategy. Nixon acceded to congressional pressure to increase welfare, food stamps, Social Security, and disability pension, and partly as a result government transfer payments to individuals rose much more during Nixon's presidency than they had during Johnson's, while growth in government social-welfare employment leveled off. In effect, the government began cutting off the route of escape from the ghettos that so many had used in the sixties: government jobs. Simply giving out money doesn't get people out. From the time Nixon took office, the black rate of exit from poverty slowed to a standstill" (Lemann, part 2, 1989 p. 28).

"The Negro poor having become more openly violent—especially in the form of the rioting of the mid 1960's—they have given the black middle class an incomparable weapon with which to threaten white America. This has been for many an intoxicating experience. 'Do this or the cities will burn.' And of course they have been greatly encouraged in this course by white rhetoric of the Kerner Commission variety. But most important of all, the existence of a large marginal, if not dependent, black urban lower class has at least given the black middle class an opportunity to establish a secure and rewarding power base in American society as the provider of social services to the black lower class.... What building contracts and police graft were to the 19th century urban Irish, the welfare department, Head Start programs and Black Studies programs will be to the coming generation of Negroes. They are of course very wise in this respect. These are expanding means of economic opportunity. By contrast, black business enterprise offers relatively little. In all this there will be the peculiar combination of weakness and strength that characterizes Negro Americans as a group at this time" (Lemann, part 2, 1989 pp. 28–29).

An income strategy was the choice that was followed but not necessarily the most effective one. "Choosing an income strategy as the means to help the ghettos would palliate poor blacks' material needs without encouraging their integration into the larger society. It was the best possible course in terms of defanging the 'militant middle class,' but not in terms of the health of black America. Moynihan chose to make the intellectual gesture rather than pursue the most effective policy" (Lemann, part 2, 1989 p. 29).

"Even more than Nixon realized, a moment had passed in American history. Race remained, and will remain, one of the obsessive themes of American life, but the period when it was the central domestic concern of the federal government was over. Partly because the Democratic Party had embraced civil rights with fervor, the presidential electorate had become essentially Republican. Even among liberals, race now had to share the agenda with other issues, like environmentalism and feminism. Watergate would quickly end Nixon's ability to make any domestic policy at all, and more important, the OPEC Oil embargo would erase the national feeling that there was enough economic breathing space to allow for the contemplation of expensive social reforms" (Lemann, part 2, 1989 p. 29).

Hence, during the course of Nixon's second term in office, the federal government was taking steps that would dismantle the War on Poverty. Whatever had happened in the past to help the disenfranchised was being dismantled. In addition, as this began a period where social welfare programs would begin to cut back, the special education laws were coming into sharp focus, which has served to assist another disenfranchised group through better educational opportunities, but the timing financially was poor, and when PL 94-142 was enacted as law in 1975, the downturn was already in progress and the law was never fully funded.

CHAPTER 11

As stated earlier, Dr. Kenneth B. Clark was one of the reigning intellectuals during the Kennedy-Johnson era of liberal reform, having achieved prominence by coordinating the testimony in *Brown v. Board of Education*, which shattered the legal foundations underpinning segregation (*Matlin*, July 17, 2014).

"Clark, who died in 2005, remains for historians a 'symbol of integrationism,' 'the civil rights movement's reigning academic,' and 'the epitome of the establishment social scientist' during the Kennedy-Johnson era of liberal reform. His credentials as a pillar of the postwar liberal establishment are plain to see. A tenured professor at the City College of New York, Clark served as an expert witness before courts and congressional committees and at White House conferences, fraternized with politicians and their advisors, and secured federal and municipal grants to support his research and activism. Those credentials and aura of respectability, were only underlined in 1969 when Clark was elected to serve as the first black president of the American Psychological Association, one of the nation's largest professional bodies.

"And yet, the remarkable controversy that ensued during Clark's presidency is a forgotten story—one that casts his life and thought in a dramatically different light, and reveals much about the pressures and dilemmas that have confronted generations of African American intellectuals. On September 4, 1971, at the end of his term in office, Clark rose to deliver his presidential address at the APA's annual convention in Washington, D.C. Within days, he had been ridiculed in the national press, denounced by many of his academic peers, and censured by the vice president of the United States" (*Matlin*, July 17, 2014).

The article went on to state that Clark was quoted as having said that he did not deliberately choose to devote his life to the problems of race and would like perhaps to escape it. His speech at the end of his term was rooted in deep disillusionment. He had higher hopes from the liberal political leadership of the 1960s, and his speech was an act of rebellion (*Matlin*, July 17, 2014). He and his fellow intellectuals of color had been cast into a role where they were "heard best when speaking to blackness" (*Matlin*, 2014, p. 2).

His larger commitment was to the pursuit of social justice. "From 1962 to 1964, with federal and New York City funding grants, Clark had designed and led a huge investigation into social and psychological conditions in Harlem, and created a blueprint for the major antipoverty initiative Harlem Youth Opportunities Unlimited known as HARYOU.

"In his book Dark Ghetto. Published in 1965 and partially serialized in the New York Post, he addressed the findings of that investigation to a general audience. Having grown up in Harlem, Clark explained, he brought the personal perspective of a long-time 'prisoner within the ghetto' to bear on the cold statistics of poverty, malnutrition, housing deprivation, infant mortality, educational failure, police brutality, criminality and addiction that were the 'objective' characteristics of ghetto experience. He wished to convey the 'subjective' dimensions of the lives from which those statistics were extracted, namely 'resentment, hostility, despair, apathy, self-deprecation, and its ironic companion, compensatory grandiose behavior" (*Matlin*, 2014, p. 3). He had ambitious plans for Haryou, calling for a $118 million budget over three years, which would rejuvenate the neighborhood's infrastructure. This was fueled by the Johnson administration's announcement of a Federal War on Poverty. As stated earlier, this program was never fully funded, and the federal initiative was not well thought out with not enough money provided to pursue the work effectively and empirically (so that programs would be researched, proved, or disproved to be successful and modified accordingly). Clark believed that only active rebellion against injustice would "free the native from his inferiority complex." These are the words of Dr. Frantz Fanon, a psychiatrist who wrote a book well-known to black power activists, *The Wretched of the Earth*, but unlike Dr. Fanon, who advocated violence against the oppressor, he believed that the "strength to rebel" could be channeled into nonviolent socially regenerative forms (*Matlin*, 2014).

The fallacy in this thinking is that a liberal government would stimulate the growth of a power organization (no matter how liberal) that would make its life uncomfortable. As a result, "maximum feasible participation (by the people who resided in the community) threatened existing political power bases and patronage networks and was quickly supplanted by traditional bureaucratic models of social service provision" (*Matlin*, 2014).

The first casualty to Haryou of this inevitable political reality was the clashing between Clark and Harlem's charismatic congressman and major powerbroker, the Reverend Adam Clayton Powell Jr., who was less than enthused by the threat of neighborhood mobilization to his power base. "By 1964, he [Powell] was pressuring Clark to merge HARYOU, at the point when it would become operational, with a local youth employment program called ACT (Associated Community Teams) that was run by his own allies. The operational management of HARYOU-ACT, Powell explained to Clark, would be directed by Livingstone Wingate—who happened to be Powell's former congressional aide" (*Matlin*, 2014).

Dr. Clark was suspicious from the outset, but he had to deal with Powell, who chaired the congressional committee through which the antipoverty legislation and any appropriations to Haryou would pass. Clark, however, believed that he could use his good standing with then Attorney General Robert F. Kennedy and his staff to force Powell to back down. However, Powell knew and was correct in believing that Kennedy would be of no assistance at a time when he was considering his run for election as US senator from New York (he could not afford to alienate the congressman from Harlem) (*Matlin*, 2014, p. 4).

"Clark was quickly forced out of the organization he had founded. A year after HARYOU-ACT came into being, the neighborhood boards that had been central to Clark's vision of community mobilization had strangely failed to materialize. Over the following years, Clark watched with deepening dismay as the federal government retreated from its commitment to the War on Poverty and escalated the War in Vietnam. The increasingly brutal, militarized suppression of urban riots of the late 1960's prompted dark reflections from Clark that America's ghettos were 'concentration camps.' 'It seems as if America has found the trick to get the Negroes to kill themselves so that they can stand before the world as superior to the German Nazis.' He added, "If I sound bitter, it is only because I am'" (*Matlin*, p. 4).

When he ascended to the APA presidency in 1969, it was a welcome validation from the professional community, yet it generated anxiety about what he would say at the presidential address at the end of his term. He made an astonishing claim in his frustration. Standing before the assembled ranks of the nation's psychologists, he said, "All power-controlling leaders should be required to accept and use the earliest perfected form of psychotechnological, biochemical intervention which would assure their use of positive power and block the possibility of their using their power destructively." This theme of using medication to control aggressive impulses was consistent with the lectures he gave at City College. During the early 1970s, when I was a student and in one of his classes, Clark took the position that sociopathy was a medical condition and therefore could best be treated by medication. Sociopaths are often the individuals who are seen conducting gang violence in the inner city, and this implied that people could not have a change in conscience because it was genetically predetermined.

"What is striking about the speech Clark delivered is not only its abrupt and disturbing prescription, but also the rationale Clark offered for his advocacy of an 'era of psychotechnology.' 'The invention of nuclear weaponry,' he explained, 'confronts us with the fact that it is now possible to destroy the human species through the nonadaptive use of human intelligence and the destructive, pathetic use of social power.' Religion, philosophy, education, and law had seemed adequate tools for controlling human destructiveness in a 'pre-nuclear age,' but were wholly inadequate now that the technology of war magnified exponentially the devastation that could be wrought by irrational or 'barbaric' acts. Only the development of drugs to counteract 'negative and primitive behavioral tendencies' would assure human survival, he insisted" (*Matlin,* 2014, p. 5).

Dr. Clark appeared to raise the bar to discussion of nuclear holocaust as his warnings about the explosive nature of the inner city was not substantial enough to grab the attention of the political leaders who could have an impact, and so he broadened his concept of explosion to include those leaders who had the power to annihilate the human race if they gave into their more primitive instincts and allowed aggression to color good judgment.

"It was Clark's own, direct encounters with political power that had crushed his hopes most profoundly, condemning his vision of a transformation of Harlem and the nation's other 'dark ghettos.'

"Johnson's military escalation and Richard Nixon's arrival in the White House had both dented Clark's faith in America's political leadership after his optimism of the early 1960's. Yet it was Clark's own, direct encounters with political power—the 'lessons' adminis-tered by Powell and, indirectly, Robert Kennedy—that had crushed his hopes most profoundly, condemning his vision of transformation of Harlem and the nation's other 'dark ghettos.' Beneath the Johnson administration's rhetoric of 'daring innovative liberalism,' he wrote in 1969, was the reality that 'canny political leadership—national and city—never intended fundamental societal reorganization.' There was to be no 'serious sharing of power'" (*Matlin*, 2014,).

PART III

The Interviews

CHAPTER 12

My DISSERTATION, WHICH IS A study conducted as part of my doctoral studies so that I would be granted my PhD in school psychology, was entitled "The Role of School Psychologists in the History of Special Education in the Commonwealth of Pennsylvania" (Weistuch 1987). This was a historical dissertation that involved poring over many documents and conducting many interviews of those who were there at the time that historical milestones in Pennsylvania occurred as it pertained to the history of special education. As stated earlier, I received my PhD from the Pennsylvania State University; hence, the history traced development in the Commonwealth of Pennsylvania. Without going through the details of my dissertation, I will discuss one part of this document as it pertains to the development of the Association for Retarded Citizens (ARC).

Before legislation is passed by the federal government, it is usually based on landmark legal cases in the States, and these result in congressional hearings and the development of law, which is then enacted. In Pennsylvania, the landmark case that was part of the ultimate Federal Law 94-142—The Education for all Handicapped Children Act of 1975—was PARC (*The Pennsylvania Association for Retarded Citizens v. PA*).

The Pennsylvania Association for Retarded Citizens grew out of the national association, which was founded in 1949. The organization was founded because parents of retarded citizens perceived that they and their children were not getting the services that they needed. Physicians and other professionals at that time frequently advised parents to place their children in institutions immediately after birth as there were no other alternatives for the care and training of these children.

Parents felt it frustrating and demoralizing that many professionals were very pessimistic about the development of retarded infants. The major needs at that time leading to the parents banding together were (1) for mutual support, (2) to educate professionals about the child's potential, and (3) for improved educational programs. This information was provided by Dr. Elton Atwater during an interview for my dissertation (Weistuch 1987). He was a political science professor at Penn State who had great difficulty securing services for his mentally retarded son. Parents took a key role in educating professionals about the possibilities, and a local chapter of PARC in State College (where Penn State is located) funded a special preschool program until classes became available. Sometimes at that time, distant residential placements were required.

In 1971, Dennis Haggerty, Esq., initiated a lawsuit as he too had a son for whom he could not secure services easily, and he had become a member of PARC. The suit was entered as *PARC v. the Commonwealth of Pennsylvania* and was a class action suit to obtain educational programming and right to due process in the Commonwealth of Pennsylvania for these disenfranchised youngsters (Weistuch 1987).

As a young doctoral student, it was intimidating to interview this man who had a beautiful office in Philadelphia and pictures on the wall showing him shaking hands with President Lyndon Johnson (it may have been after his presidency as the legislation was post his administration). He was a nice man, however, and offered information about the case and its outcome. Mr. Haggerty, before the suit, became involved with the PARC Committee on State Hospitals in 1967, which was one year after Robert Kennedy laid open the wound in New York regarding Willowbrook. Mr. Kennedy was the US senator from New York at that time and made it a legislative issue after the report by Geraldo Rivera.

Mr. Haggerty began to bring people into the state institutions, and at that time in 1969, another attorney whose brother was in Whitehaven School and Hospital, Mr. Thomas Gilhool, presented a case with ARC about the hideous conditions at Pennhurst and other state schools in Pennsylvania. They were going to fight in the courts on behalf of retarded citizens about several issues including architectural barriers (these types of issues are ultimately what led to ramps and handicapped bathrooms as well as handicapped parking spaces), right to education, and right to treatment.

The educational issue was addressed first as it was the easiest to define. The definition of education's help by PARC was a simplistic one—it did not have to be addition, subtraction, etc.—it might be tying a shoe or recognition of colors. The state's case was going badly, and they entered into a consent agreement with PARC. This would avoid the continuation of a long drawn-out court case as the parties agreed to settle by offering PARC what they sought.

Programs for the severely and profoundly mentally retarded were offered statewide as a result of this case (Weistuch 1987).

This is the landmark case that I can talk fluently about, although there were others throughout the United States. The result was PL 94-142, which was the Education for Handicapped Children Act signed into federal law by President Gerald R. Ford in 1975. The results of this law led to many classes for children who were less handicapped, as well as classes for the learning disabled in greater abundance than had been the case beforehand. Most notably, parents had due process, and children could not be placed in special education classes unless the local educational entity met with the parents and discussed their findings from evaluations conducted by the school and a specialized program (individualized educational program, or IEP, was created and signed by the parents) prior to the child's entry into the program.

Very significantly, parents had a right to be involved in their child's education, and the schools could no longer test and place children without parental permission. After the testing, the family would meet with the schools, and the school would state whether the child was eligible for a special education program. More was also done to educate teachers so that there would be fewer biases and statements about "tard classes." However, although less cruel, it has been my experience since special education teachers are trained separately from regular education teachers that regular education teachers still have a fear of involving special needs students in their classes. They are undertrained many times about these students.

This had become a major problem with the process that came out of the new laws, which is called mainstreaming. Mainstreaming is a process whereby students, when they are ready, are given opportunities in their strongest areas to be educated with students who are not handicapped (in general or regular education). Although it has become far better, my experience is that these mainstream opportunities need to be well managed. If you just place a child in this type of class experience without preparing them, the regular education teacher and the children in the classroom are often less than accepting of the special needs student (unless the children are very young), and it can be a horrible experience for the special needs student. This is not always managed well, although it is far better than it had been in the past.

CHAPTER 13

THE BOOK AS A WHOLE is about those people who have been given fewer opportunities in the United States because of the underspending of money where it is needed by those most underserved by the United States government. I do not believe that this situation will change substantially enough because of the political wrangling that takes place in this country. It is possible, as I will suggest later, that private funding can work to resolve many of these problems and the shortfall of funds that have been made available for the "have-nots" in this country, whether due to special needs, birth in an impoverished area, immigration to the United States with limited or no resources, etc. The interviews are dealing with those who have needed special education services in school and unfortunately have not received, at least without a fight, needed services or those who have been intruded upon by a government agency who has not fairly understood the needs of the family due to lack of trained personnel, etc. In either case, it is the lack of funding in critical functions of the government that perpetuates these problems.

The next chapters of this book will be focused on special education. Interviews have been conducted with families who have had to struggle with these issues and have had to fight to get their child's needs met. These fights come up as 94-142, which, I have been discussing, was never fully funded. The lack of funding by the government has once again led to people who need services for completion of their education, and the families have to fight for this as these services that their children need have not readily been provided despite promises to the contrary.

One limitation of this book is that I have been able to interview those individuals who have made the funds available to either fight on their own or engage an attorney to litigate on behalf of their special needs child. In the inner city, it is often the case that parents do not have the funding, and there is nothing they can do to fight the district. In fact, I have heard from more than one special education attorney that the district will count on the fact that they can intimidate parents into submission in this type of situation, knowing that most parents cannot afford to fight them.

With this limitation stated, I proceeded to interview three families about issues they encountered in special education and the wrangling they needed to go through to get their kids' needed services. The next page will show the release signed by all those interviewed whether related to special education or Child Protective Services. It acknowledges that the origin of the interviews (area where the family resides, names of the principals, etc.) will not be revealed. It also indicated that I am writing this book with journalistic and historical interest and not in my role as a psychologist. After sharing this release, I will offer the interviews that took place with the families described.

NORMAN WEISTUCH, PhD

RELEASE FORM

It is understood that Dr. Norman Weistuch is writing a book entitled *A Kid from the Bronx*.

He is interviewing individuals who are relevant to the material within the book re: Child Protective Services or Special Education. These interviews are being conducted for the purposes of journalism and are documenting events for Dr. Weistuch to this end and not in his role as a licensed psychologist. Dr. Weistuch will not use names, locations, or other data from the interview to identify those interviewed and will make every effort to maintain the anonymity of those interviewed (keep their identities unknown).

To this end, I, _____, am giving my permission to include any interview in the book mentioned above.

_____

Interviewee

Dr. Weistuch

CHAPTER 14

ONE OF THE FAMILIES INTERVIEWED has a son who is now an adult. When he attended school in the younger grades (currently involved in graduate studies), he was diagnosed with multiple disabilities including Asperger's disorder, severe anxiety, and a reading disability.

At the younger ages, because of his disability, he was in a self-contained classroom (which means all his work was with one special education teacher and the other students in the classroom had similar disabilities). His school career in this classroom went well. However, when he became middle-school age, the school district wanted to mainstream him (as stated earlier, this is a program where the disabled student in classes where he or she is stronger are placed in subject classes in the areas of strength with nondisabled students).

The parents did not want their son mainstreamed. He was still several years behind in reading and getting individualized reading instruction daily. In middle school, each class was departmentalized, and their son would have to go from class to class, and he was not yet educationally or emotionally equipped to do this. They were also not addressing the reading problem adequately enough. Even though he was getting individualized reading help, although I did not ask the parents this question, it might have been that it was with the wrong techniques, which often happens, and I am not sure what the reasons are why the parents felt the instruction was not adequate in reading, but they were close to the situation and had their reasons. It might have also been that when the child was to be mainstreamed, they would remove the current reading program and expect that he would do well in the regular classroom without this instruction.

Parents who seek out the right services are the best to assess how their child is doing, which is why there is now due process so that parents have the right to approve or not their child's program, and clearly the parents likely did make good choices as the educational program was modified and their child, who is now an adult, is involved in graduate studies, which is a tribute to the student and the parents.

When the student was to be mainstreamed and the parents disputed this program, this was when they sought legal action. The teacher at this time wanted the parents to work with their son on reading at home, saying, "Just do what you can." The assignments were not appropriate, and this was a serious problem. When the family sat down at the IEP meeting (individualized education plan, which is required by law for every classified student), and they were not getting the program they wanted, the parents felt it was best to take him out of the school and place him unilaterally (this means without the school district's agreement, and the financial responsibility to pay for the school becomes the parent's) in a special school program because the district was dragging their feet. As stated earlier, it is very fortunate for this young man that his parents were both working at good jobs and had the means to pay for the program. This is often not the case in the inner city, and the parents are often stuck with whatever school program the district requires, and the family often in this situation does not have the financial resources to either fight with an attorney who is very expensive or pay for an out-of-district special school, which is also very expensive.

In this case, the judge, according to the parents, seemed to be biased toward the school district, and the parents decided to give up the litigation because of the expense; instead, they spent the money on the special school program. The psychologist on the team (who make the decisions about special education programming) even openly admitted he had not read the last triennial report (it is required in most states that children be reevaluted by the team in order to continue classification and either maintain or modify the child's program) and had no intention despite any evidence to the contrary of making any changes in their child's program in the direction that the parents might have wanted.

By the time the child had reached high school age, he made enough progress in reading to be mainstreamed into the district high school. Although, this youngster had a difficult time at first making the transition, including openly having tantrums in the halls in frustration, the psychologist at the high school worked closely with a private psychologist hired by the parents, as well as a psychiatrist, who provided the medical, educational, and social support to make this experience work for this young man. Even to the point that the private psychologist was hired over a two-year period by the district to create a social skills group involving this young man and several of his peers who met on a weekly basis to discuss some of their issues and frustrations related to interacting with others at the high school and also having a component where once a month the students went out with the psychologist and some of the parents to local places to have fun, such as a place with pinball, video games, and miniature golf, so they could socialize and bond together as a group.

The district, according to the parents, would not do the right thing for this child, which usually occurs because of the expense. However, as stated, fortunately in this situation, the parents had the means to help this child despite the district. In an urban area where money is an issue for the parents, the outcome here could have been very different.

CHAPTER 15

AN INTERVIEW WAS CONDUCTED WITH a second family who also has a son who is now an adult where there were issues dealing with their school system. Their son had severe anxiety. He did not want to go to school, and he was in the nurse's office every day. He would not eat as he feared he was going to choke. He was later diagnosed with obsessive-compulsive disorder. He did not socialize with other kids, and his family kept him back a year and the family saw many psychologists.

The family, fortunately for them and for their son, had the means to test their son privately. The team from the school district refused to evaluate. The teachers were cooperating with the family and showed concern about their son. Eventually, the school district agreed to send their son to an out-of-district placement that could more properly address his needs.

Their son remained in out-of-district school placement for the remainder of his school life, but the school district never fully understood what their son needed. There were periods of time where the family had to pay for an advocate to help them, as the school district kept looking to return him to the district. He was hospitalized at one point, and he went to a hospital school program, yet the school district, without the help of outside professionals and advocacy, persisted in their push to bring him back in district despite the fact that he was home half the time as he often refused to go to school.

With the help of the family and outside mental health and medical professionals, the family, despite the efforts on the part of the school district, kept him in the programs and services he needed, and their son is now age thirty, living independently, and has a job. Although the family provides some financial support, they are proud of him because he created a life for himself.

CHAPTER 16

AN INTERVIEW WAS HELD WITH one parent who has a son, currently age sixteen. He is successful now, but getting things to this point led to numerous battles with the school district in which he is enrolled.

The mother of this child was interviewed and stated that her son was diagnosed with attention deficit hyperactivity disorder (ADHD) and oppositional defiant disorder (ODD) at age two. Although the child was diagnosed early, he suffered throughout his preschool years at the whim of private day cares, since the income of the family was too high to qualify for a free preschool program. Due to aggressive behaviors, the child attended five preschools due to his expulsion from four of these programs. Right before kindergarten, he was able to stay at a preschool because the owner of the preschool kept strict discipline and was determined to make it work.

Because of the behavioral difficulties during her son's preschool years, the mother called a meeting with her son's new school several months prior to the start of kindergarten. She was determined that kindergarten would be better than preschool had been for her, so she assembled her own team: a psychologist, a psychiatrist (for medication management), and an advocate. Armed with documentation from her team and one from one of the day cares that had expelled him and the advocate by her side, she approached the school, requesting an aide for her son to guide him and head off any behavior problems in school. She shared her son's diagnosis at age two and the extensive testing that the renowned hospital that evaluated him had provided. There was additional information provided by these reports that could have helped her son, but a school district always has the option to accept or reject outside reports. In this situation, their school district rejected the outside reports in favor of their own evaluations. This lost the family the aide they requested that would have helped him so much during his most difficult time, kindergarten through grade 2.

Instead, the school district conducted its own evaluation of her son. He was classified as meeting the criteria for educational accommodations based upon the school's testing. He began with a 504v Plan (nonspecial education accommodations), though the family had requested an IEP (individualized education plan), which is a special education program. As previously noted, the family's request for an aide was denied. This led to many problems at school for him due to his aggressive behaviors, such as hitting other children and throwing rocks at them. It also led to many parent-teacher conferences and several school suspensions and detentions for the child. Because of these problems, the following year, the school allowed an IEP, but no aide.

By the time her son was approaching second grade, he had been suspended several times and had several detentions as mentioned earlier. Grade 1 had been especially challenging, despite Mom's frequent involvement volunteering at school, her new part-time work status, her frequent contacts with the child's teachers, and the parents' constant support at home. So when the school met for his annual IEP meeting, the principal of this child's elementary school had requested testing for autism, as she appeared determined to have the child placed in a special school.

According to his mother, what the school was requesting was inappropriate, since she knew that the hospital's diagnosis of ADHD and ODD was correct. Also, a parent knows her child best, and she saw no signs of autism. The school conducted their own autism testing by administering one test to the teacher and the mother, and the parents were forced to accept the results. (This is the standard practice in the special education system.) Due to inconclusive testing data to classify the child as autistic, the school district made modifications to keep him in the regular classroom.

During grade 3, things eased a bit when the family switched to a behavioral pediatrician Mom had found through her involvement in CHADD, a parent support group for children with ADHD. This provider was able to provide superior medication management for her son's condition. Additionally, the family found a therapist who worked with them and directly with their son, not just the parents. However, it had to be paid for out of pocket and not through insurance. This therapist was able to set up the best behavioral program possible for their son, including his becoming aware of social cues. These supports, the behavioral pediatrician and the therapist, significantly eased her son's anxiety in school.

In her son's early years, this parent was concerned that her career was in jeopardy, given the many day care programs he was removed from and the amount of time she needed to make available to make sure her son was able to access his educational program. Her son seemed to require more time than her even new part-time schedule would allow. This situation boiled over when her son was approximately eight years old and she had to split care between three caregivers when the part-time day care at his elementary school refused service because of her child's aggressive behavior. She worried she might have to quit her job to care for her son.

The next major event in her son's school struggles occurred when her son entered grade 8 and other issues with anxiety began to emerge. This came to a head in grade 9 when he took an advanced placement (AP) class and was diagnosed with obsessive-compulsive disorder (OCD). His anxiety was flaring up, so he had daily meltdowns about doing homework. However, the special education teacher refused to help because he was not doing poorly in school (had straight As). Mom requested a 504 meeting (he no longer had an IEP), which she and Dad attended. The meeting was abortive, though, as the school again refused to respond to the parents' request for help. He also needed extended time to be granted for the AP test. However, the request was not granted, and the district was unsupportive. Her son took the AP exam but did not pass the test. Therefore, the school failed the family because of the outcome.

At this point, her son is succeeding, but it has been very difficult and provided more work on the part of the mother than should have been necessary to work around the school district's continued lack of support.

CHAPTER 17

ONE FINAL INTERVIEW WAS HELD with a family who had issues about special education and their daughter. The mother of this family was interviewed. She has three children who are currently adults. Her two eldest boys were diagnosed during the school years: ADHD—combined type (older son) and ADHD—inattentive type (middle son). Although her youngest daughter as a child would rock on a rocking horse for long periods of time, there was nothing of major concern identified by Mom or the school in her early years.

In second grade, it was noted that instead of attending to school-work, her daughter would become distracted (and they lived in a more rural area) and look at the baby cows outside. As she became older, she had a hard time concentrating.

By grade 7, this youngster was having many issues in school. She was getting detention all the time due to inattention in class, and she was beginning to act out in school. At that time (which is now known to be false), it was believed that by age thirteen, kids would "grow out of ADD." It was also believed by many parents that it was only boys (although it is factual that a higher percentage of boys are diagnosed with ADD).

The mother went on to describe that a friend and her daughter got together, and the mother of this friend (whose daughter had been diagnosed with ADD and was taking Ritalin) asked this mom if her daughter was taking Ritalin. The mom interviewed did not believe, because she was a girl, that her daughter could have ADD. The doctor never said anything, the school never said anything, but her daughter kept getting in trouble at school.

For example, while in grade 7, her daughter could not get through one of the books she was assigned to read, Pet Sematary (King, 1983), because of her difficulty with attention and distractibility, so instead, she watched the movie. She wrote the report based on the movie and did well until her teacher found out that she had not read the book. At this point, her grade was changed to D.

Ultimately, Mom brought her daughter to a psychologist after it was discovered by the girl's brother that this twelve-year0old was plotting train times near their home and was thinking of throwing herself in front of a train. She was finally at this time diagnosed with symptoms of ADHD and depression and placed on medication. It was also a problem at school that the officials in the district as well as teachers would think that this young lady was acting (as she had significant problems with attendance) when she was having an asthma attack. On one occasion, the vice principal saw them taking the young lady out on a stretcher to a waiting ambulance because of an asthma attack, and the school tried to give her detention because she missed eighth-period class (this was the period that was to happen at the time she was being taken to a waiting ambulance).

It is also well-known at this time that kids with ADHD have difficulties with sleep and getting up in the morning. On at least one occasion, this youngster, by this point, based on the way she was being treated, wanted to get under their skin, reluctantly came to school (she would often come in late due to her difficulty getting up) but brought her pillow along.

Finally, due to the issues with emotion, behavior, and ADHD, the team at her local school district evaluated and classified her. She received resource room support for study skills and in-class support in some subject areas. In-class support means that she would be in classes where there was both a regular and special education teacher, and she was entitled to support from the special education teacher when needed. Resource room is a pull-out program, where, in her case, she received study skill support in a special class. These services, when her mom allowed me to look at her individualized education plan (IEP), revealed that she was entitled to these services from grade 7 through high school graduation.

However, because of lack of motivation and behaviors, she received more suspensions than assistance from the district according to her mom. Except for outside services (psychological and psychiatric support), the family felt they received limited support from the school district and more punitive actions, such as suspensions, detentions, and accusations. At one point she was accused of "being a druggie." There was never any documentation that she used drugs, and she never smoked cigarettes because of her asthma.

According to her mom, this young lady's support was from her parents and outside support, and the family felt no sense of support from the school district she attended, although she did ultimately graduate.

A last example given by this mom also happened in seventh grade. This youngster had a fight with her math teacher (they did not get along with each other). She was brought to the guidance office and told she would not be allowed to go back to her math class until she apologized to her teacher. As has already been discussed, this young lady tended to be unmoved, if not defiant, when required by school personnel to do something, and she refused to cooperate. She remained in the guidance office (since it was already May) for the remainder of the school year.

It was about this time (May of her seventh-grade year) that she was evaluated for classification. Her mom pointed out to the school that there was no air-conditioning in the classroom (as there was in the guidance office) and a teacher with whom she did not get along. There was no incentive for her daughter to apologize when she could do her work, not interact with the teacher, and stay in air-conditioning if she stood her ground. Her mom said there was not an attempt on the part of the school to try to work it out with the student and her teacher by sitting down with both. Instead, the school was trying to force her to apologize, yelled at her, and cast blame.

According to Mom, the school at their best worked with her two sons (both of whom had ADHD) very effectively. However, because her daughter tended to be more defiant, the school did not handle this well.

CHAPTER 18

As can be seen from the last few chapters, there have been many issues related to special education and the schools fulfilling their mandate. I am persuaded that with the optimism of 94-142, the Education for All Handicapped Children Act of 1975, that the fact that the federal government has never fully funded the enactment of this law (which went into effect in October 1977), the problems discussed in the previous chapters were an inevitable outcome. As stated earlier, it is even worse in the inner city where the chance to even begin to solve these problems fails because many parents have given up as they do not have the financial resources to challenge the public school on behalf of their children. Providing the proper funding for the special education programs, in my opinion, will never be remedied to the extent needed unless private funding is opened as a door to provide for this gap in services.

I will now be turning my attention to another system, which has been woefully flawed. As stated earlier, there have been many discussions and efforts to provide better opportunities for people in the inner city. Families have been terribly hurt in many instances not only by the gap in services seen in the schools with respect to special education but also by the terrible inequities related to Child Protective Services and its role in the state to attempt to provide protection for children against abuse and neglect. Although the mission is praiseworthy, the implementation has been notably flawed.

To begin this section of the book, I was fortunate to have had the opportunity to interview Allison C. Williams, Esq. She has defended many families in situations where the Division of Child Protection and Permanency (Child Protective Services in the state of

New Jersey) has overreached its bounds and created major problems for those families who have sought her services.

Ms. Williams stated during the interview that she founded the firm to help families deal with Child Protective Services and specifically to address child protection in cases where the agency (1) comes up with solutions, which do not fit the family; (2) commences an investigation and does nothing to help children in need; or (3) overstep its bounds and harasses a family when it is unnecessary.

The division often determines that is has identified the problem, and even where there is no mental health history, they will ask for psychological evaluations, substance abuse evaluations, and expend much time and unnecessary resources so they can document what they have done in court. An abundance of "services," even those ill-fitted to a family's needs, helps the division to persuade judges that they have exhausted all "reasonable efforts" to help a family, when in fact they have caused further delay in reunification or, worse, created a paper trail to bolster a request to terminate parental rights for parents whose identified needs were simply incorrect.

There is a middle ground where they identify the problem of the child and services do not address the problem and do not help to resolve it. It may be that the school does not want to pay for services (child study team), and ultimately there is a lack of fitness determined on the part of the parents because the problem is not being addressed by the parents (coded as neglect). Ms. Williams will take on cases where the family takes their often limited resources to invest in an attorney so they do not have to secure representation from the public defender.

The firm tends to see more complex cases: Munchausen by proxy, undiagnosed mental health disorders, substance abuse disorders, and child sexual abuse, for example. There will be a checklist offered of services that the family needs to secure, and the services may not be on point, but the division must allay its own fears by requesting services that may not be needed.

Some settlements in court include issues that involve the parent continuing to have contact with the child, but they can only do so at home. The question becomes, if the mother (or father) is so dangerous, why can she (he) have contact with the child at home only? This situation, for example, may be created when there is a contentious divorce, and the father (or mother) wants control of the situation so he (she) controls the situation by not permitting the mother (or father) to leave the home with the children (i.e., fear of kidnapping, etc.). This may allay the dad's (or mom's) fears and may make the division feel better that they have addressed the dad's (or mom's) concerns, but such a restriction may be totally unnecessary.

The agency (DCP and P) will often send a list of services needed to large agencies, and the parents may not have mental health issues. The word comes back from the agency that the services have "solved the problem," when in essence there may have been no problem to begin with, and "magically" the family gets better. Everyone attributes it to the services and DCP and P intervention, when in fact services had nothing to do with it.

In one case, a mother was eight months pregnant, and there were three other kids in the family. The father was removed from the home in a divorce case because she was injured, and he was the "abuser" despite the fact that they were both mildly abusive to each other. He was barred from the home, but the mom stated she needed help with the children. This created enormous stress on the family as he was labeled an "abuser" and thus had to leave the home.

There have also been cases where a family has an autistic child, and the family is sent to parenting classes. What is a garden-variety parenting class going to teach a parent about handling an autistic child? In some cases, anger management classes are offered with a set twenty-six-week course provided in a group setting: How does this compare to therapy, which is offered through insurance by a licensed professional—group or individual where the licensed professional plans the service to meet the individual needs of the client referred? Individual therapy is very different than the twenty-six-week model, where there is no planning about the people in the group, which can range from those dealing with extreme violence to those where there are minor infractions, and yet, they are in the same group.

Another problem surrounds dealing with the Regional Diagnostic Treatment Centers (RDTC). These child abuse centers will have a multidisciplinary team approach where multiple professionals each conduct an evaluation on multiple members of the family and piece their description of an individual family member into a joint report. The people doing the evaluations are often licensed clinical social workers, and the director signs off on the report without ever seeing the family (the director is the psychologist). The reports are often poorly worded with inflammatory comments, and the labels applied are often by those who are not trained to diagnose and often miss the mark. A small part of the problem may be about the label applied, and the reports carry enormous weight with little substance to back it up. Then the psychologist (director) is often the person testifying in court as the expert witness when he has only signed off on the report but did not actually see the family. Thus, the parent loses all ability to confront the testifying witness with his personal observations of the parent or child and the context in which certain statements were made.

In one case, a husband was accused of sexual abuse of his daughter, and the division started "leaning on Mom" to separate from the dad. Ultimately, the child (age four) recanted. There was a civil finding that the father had abused the child. DCP and P would not allow the father to see either of his kids, including a son who made no allegation of abuse. The court denied the application for even supervised visits. The father lost his job after being accused of sexual abuse, and the mother had to change her shift so she could work during the day (loss of income compared with her night hours). The mother went to a "head hunter (job recruiter)" who found her a job out of state, but the judge would not let Mom leave the state even though there was lost income to the family. The therapy that was provided to the child was really used to pressure the child to recant her recantation (recanting means that the child who had originally accused the parent of sexual abuse stated at a later time that this did not happen). The child became distressed because nobody believed her. When the mother brought to the court's attention the pressure placed on the child in therapy, the court punished the mom by placing the kids in foster care. This is where judges and DCP and P use their power to "demolish" people.

A planning device used by the division is the family team meeting. This is designed to bring together the agency personnel and the family and set goals allowing the client receiving DCP and P services to have "input" into their program. DCP and P often tries to exclude attorneys from these meeting, though the higher-ups at the state have finally overturned this practice because it is clear that people can be railroaded without their attorneys present.

Another loaded issue with the division involves what is referred to as "Finding Words Training." Where the allegation is sexual abuse, the caseworker is obliged to interview as if it was an investigation for any other type of complaint. If something is stated by the child that constitutes a crime (i.e., sexual abuse), the caseworker is to stop immediately and contact a prosecutor. The caseworker also needs to determine if a mental health interview should occur. At an RDTC, it may be a social worker or a psychologist, depending on who is assigned for the rotation on that day. The caseworkers, however, will often taint the testimony of the client. The caseworkers will need to ensure the child's well-being and talk in words that do not influence the child in what they say, but often, they will "grill the child," and the training they receive on how to handle these situations is limited and, hence, not effective when the situation comes up.

Another issue that is a major problem with the division is repeated placements. If the division gets a "good child," they will reward "frequent flyer foster parents" with this child. With children who have major issues, such as cognitive impairment, poverty, etc., you cannot "fix the situation" if all the blame is foisted on the parents. These children cannot be "repaired" in one year, which is the timeline for the situation to improve before children are removed from homes permanently. These problem kids bounce from place to place because they are more traumatized by being removed from their homes, and sometimes they are worse, and this could linger for years. Kids are often more traumatized by the placement process and the belief that their parents don't love them than the process could be if the child had remained at home with effective services.

CHAPTER 19

As can be seen, as in the area of special education where the Education for all Handicapped Children Act (94-142), which was signed in 1975 and never fully funded, there are also issues related to helping families once a complaint is substantiated (that they document their finding of abuse and/or neglect) by Child Protective Services and the way these situations are handled. The connection here, especially in the inner city, is about funding. The state is acting more as a watchdog about families, which serves a good purpose when removing children from dangerous situations is justified and the family is so unable to pull themselves together that ultimately adoption is warranted. However, as pointed out by Allison Williams in the last chapter, the effect on families and the way it can be handled can be devastating. Although there are many issues and interrelated agencies such as vocational services, the ability to receive proper housing for those in poverty, etc., my main focus as a mental health professional is the implementation of effective services and for the right reasons when mental health services are needed.

As stated earlier, the problems with 94-142 are again in terms of the money set aside by the federal government and the states to properly implement special education services, and without full funding, it leads to many problems as previously discussed. With respect to Child Protective Services, the issues are related to the fact that people are forced to be involved in counseling services, and it is long known in my field that forced or court-ordered services have its limitations, and certainly, the therapist must allay the fears of the client and provide effective services. For the most poor, for example, Medicaid reimbursement, which was discussed in earlier chapters, pays for many of the services; and even when private insurers are paying services, there is a great deal less covered than there used to be. The reimbursement to professionals is less than what is has been in the past, and many of the most capable professionals will not accept Medicaid because of the poor level of reimbursement offered for mental health services. The results in the case of private insurers is that the cost that the client has to pay keeps going up (copays, etc.), which can lead to a level of financial hardship on the part of clients who are forced into therapy. For those on Medicaid, often the services are poor and not up to the job required to help the family because the best specialists will not accept Medicaid reimbursement, and those left are often undertrained for the job.

The issues delineated through the course of this book are related to funding from the federal government / state government, etc., and although I myself have only been associated in my training and work experience with three states (New York, New Jersey, and Pennsylvania), since the funding streams are based on federal initiatives, these problems that have been delineated through the course of this book are nationwide. It is my hope that this book will spur many more visible complaints that see the light of day throughout the country so that we can work as a nation in repairing these issues through the raising of funds that have the capacity to help many across the nation.

For now, I would like to turn my attention to three interviews I conducted with individuals who have experienced a rough time due to their families coming to the attention of Child Protective Services. Again, I stress as one limitation of this book that I have not been able to meet and interview individuals who are in the most dire financial circumstances and had available to me only those families who had the funds or chose to gather whatever money they could to fight the findings of Child Protective Services. There are many more throughout the nation in poverty who do not have the money as is the case with fighting their local school district or Child Protective Services and need to struggle with what they are required to do without protest.

One woman who told her story spoke about Child Protective Services (and I am using this generically as each state has an agency with a different name that is assigned this function) becoming involved because her daughter and daughter's boyfriend became involved with drugs and had a child. The couple were staying with the parents of the boyfriend, and the boyfriend and his father got involved in an altercation. The police came, and because a child was involved, Child Protective Services (CPS) was called.

In the meantime, the young lady called her mother (whom I interviewed), and she came over and took the toddler who was between two and three years old at that time. In the early morning (midnight or 1:00 a.m.), CPS came to the door. They wanted to check the child to make sure the child was not hurt. CPS stayed for a while, questioning the family. Her daughter also asked if she and her boyfriend could stay with her parents because they were asked to leave the other home. She told her daughter they could stay overnight. CPS decided to award custody of the toddler to the maternal grandparents.

CPS was required to check the background of the grandparents. CPS had been involved about twenty years earlier with the grandparents about their daughter. There were accusations that were a strike against the grandfather. Their daughter had gone to an alternative high school (due to emotional/behavioral issues that were interfering with learning), and she wanted to go to a party. Her father said no. They got into an argument, and he might have slapped his daughter. CPS became involved and interviewed the family. It was dropped and forgotten because abuse was not substantiated.

When this came up during the background check, in order to retain custody of their grandson, they had to expunge the record and engaged counsel to help them. They had no documents about this long ago incident as they had not seen it as that important.

In the meantime, CPS required the grandparents to go to parenting classes, CPS took fingerprints of the grandparents, and CPS came weekly to check on the grandson. As there had been a prior incident with CPS, in order to retain custody of the grandson, the grandfather was not permitted to live in his home.

The grandfather is disabled and does not work. His mother-in-law lived with them, and she was also disabled. The grandfather was taking care of the grandson and the mother-in-law at that time until he was required to leave the home. He had to move in with his sister. The grandmother was working at that time, and she did not know what to do to provide care to her grandchild and her mother.

This grandmother cared deeply for her mother and her grandson. She also cared deeply for her husband. This grandmother felt forced into a position where she stated that in order to keep her grandson if this meant divorcing her husband, she would do this. One caseworker for CPS said, "You know we did not want to say that, but..." The grandmother was forced into a position like this and was angry.

It did end up going to court, and her husband took care of all this. She understands that this is the job of CPS but cannot understand why they were "all over her," and you hear stories of abused and neglected children where their families are not watched as closely as she was—at least in her opinion.

This went on for months. Her husband had gone away for a couple of days with his sister, but they secretly kept him at home because they did not know how to solve the care problem. This grandmother questions the stability that would have been created if she had to divorce her husband.

The way it was resolved is that CPS went to court. The caseworker then stated in court that is was resolved, and the family was permitted to go back to their normal life.

CHAPTER 20

AN INTERVIEW WAS CONDUCTED AS well with a father who described his experiences with CPS. This individual stated that he was going through a divorce, and his ex-wife consulted her lawyer. In his opinion, her lawyer had a similar case and advised her to use CPS "as a tool." Her mother came from an Eastern European country and did not speak English. Their daughters were ages eight years and eighteen months. Both mother and grandmother spoke with the teacher of the eight-year-old and alleged sexual abuse. The nurse and the principal were involved and reported their concerns to CPS. The lawyers for the two parents stopped communicating, and a caseworker from CPS came to the father's home. The caseworker stated that the mother and grandmother were sincere and stated that the father must sign off on a plan stating he could not have contact with his daughters and he could no longer reside in the marital home.

The allegations came originally from the grandmother who did not speak English. She stated through her daughter who translated what had occurred. It was stated by the grandmother that this father showered with the eighteen-month-old daughter and asked her to play with his sexual parts. There was a herpetic virus that the daughter had, and the caseworker stated to the pediatrician and in her report that these rashes were only below her waistline, which (a) was misinformation and (b) was not sexually transmitted.

There were police reports about baths or showers taking place with the little one. Bathing was his responsibility, but there was no information in the police reports suggesting inappropriate behavior. Further, the person accusing him only spoke her native language and not English.

The grandmother gave both of the girls a bath one day. It was the day before a parent mediation meeting (where the attorneys or the county—if the meeting is occurring with staff from the court where the case is being tried—get together to try to resolve the issues between the parents, interfering with the settlement of the divorce). The grandmother stated that the eight-year-old stuck her finger in the vagina of the eighteen-month-old. When the grandmother asked why she did this (and the father stated that his daughter does not speak the native language of the grandmother), the eight-year-old stated, "Daddy does it to me."

The CPS investigator interviewed the eight-year-old, who denied that the dad ever touched her inappropriately. A police investigator also interviewed the eight-year-old, and the girl again denied this ever happened. The medical and psychological evaluations also produced no positive results supporting sexual abuse. The medical doctor saw the herpetic lesions on the eighteen-month-old, and they were sampled and sent to a lab. The doctor reported that this was a medical problem, which was being treated, but that it was not sexually transmitted. The entire process took about one month, during which time this father was not able to have contact with his daughters or reside in the home.

This father moved in with a friend who had two kids, and according to the father, his ex-wife called CPS and alleged that the father was also molesting these two children. A different investigator found no evidence to support this.

The father's attorney fought back, and in court, when CPS was pressed, the investigation, which at first was coded as not established, was then coded as unfounded (i.e., that there was not enough evidence to substantiate sexual abuse).

CHAPTER 21

THE LAST CLIENT INTERVIEWED WAS a mother who teaches sports to children and teens (in order to help preserve confidentiality, this mother requested I not name the particular sport). She received a call from a CPS caseworker who asked her to leave work and come home. However, she had responsibility for many kids and could not leave. The caseworker agreed to meet her at her place of work. The parent asked if she needed a lawyer, and the caseworker said no, that she just needed to sign some papers regarding her kids.

This mother was a coach to a girl whose mother was very sick and wheelchair bound. Unfortunately, the mother who was sick passed away. The mother I interviewed got to know this family, and she began dating the father after his wife passed away. One of the older daughters in the family had a history of depression and suicidal thoughts. The mother interviewed became involved in a serious relationship with this father, and she became pregnant. There were also two stepdaughters after they married, and within one year's time, she was the mother of four children.

The father renovated houses for a living and wanted to rebuild the house they were living in (so that it would be a new house and the memories of their mom would not loom). The mother interviewed wanted a big wedding, but the father wanted something simple. It was a quick wedding, and the daughter she gave birth to was christened the same weekend.

Soon after they were married, the mother realized that he was very controlling. She limited her coaching responsibilities and became a full-time mom. The stepdaughters used to fight vigorously, and as the mom gave up her coaching responsibilities, the girl she had coached became jealous that she and the mom would be spending less time together.

The father, however, stated nevertheless that he would take care of the finances and she would care for the kids. However, he considered her stepdaughters as "his kids," and the family was not being structured as a family unit. He would insult her in front of the kids. Their two little kids did not understand, but her stepdaughters clearly saw the tension.

It became over time both a verbally and physically abusive relationship. At this point, she took care of the little ones, but the older ones, after a while, were not permitted to talk to her. Her friends were embarrassed for her and started to move away from the relationship. She felt isolated.

A female friend of his was the babysitter, and she did not want to relinquish care of the little ones to the mother at the end of the day. There was no trust. The father ultimately asked for a divorce, and the sitter kept the kids at her house for an overnight. Her husband then told her that if she took the kids, the husband would have her charged with kidnapping and abandonment.

The mother then called and stated to the babysitter that she was coming to take the kids, and she told the babysitter that she was fired. She was ready to leave with the kids and go to her parents but decided to stay for fear of what might happen.

She was pushed hard by her husband at one point, and she wanted to leave their home. He tried to block her at the door, but she eventually got out of the house. She contacted the police, and a restraining order was in place after that.

He had weapons in the house, and she did not mention that when they went to court for fear he would hurt the kids. The judge rescinded the restraining order, stating it was a domestic dispute and they should go to family therapy. The family therapy was not working, and his daughters were resentful that she had placed a restraining order on their dad. At this point, the girls were thirteen and nine.

On one occasion, the mom wanted the nine-year-old to do something, and she refused. The mom sent her to her room. The second babysitter hired by the father called CPS and stated that the mom was abusive to his girls. Mom had filed for divorce by this time, and when interviewed by the caseworker, the mom stated that the weapons needed to be off the property. The caseworker at first stated that it was safe because the weapons were locked away. However, with mom's insistence, the caseworker finally asked the dad to remove them.

The caseworker kept challenging the mom with questions. Her husband, within days, went to the police. She had the kids at her parents' home for the night. The police called, stating that her husband was concerned about the whereabouts of the kids (even though she had told him where they would be staying). The husband at this point went to the court and filed for temporary sole custody, and the judge granted it.

The mom was not permitted to take the kids out of the house. The youngest daughter had tendonitis. The father needed to take her to the hospital as Mom was not permitted to leave the house with any of the kids. He took the youngest daughter and their son to the hospital. The father, however, insisted that the mother pick up their son. She refused to do this as she knew, if caught with one of their kids outside of the house, she could go to jail. Her husband knew this.

According to this mother, the CPS caseworker accused the mom of not acting in the best interest of their children for not picking up their son. There were several interviews with CPS. CPS canceled the meeting several times, yet Mom received a letter stating that she was noncompliant with the interview process. This mom felt under attack from the CPS caseworker who was challenging her parenting. The caseworker was younger than the mom and stated she had never been a parent. The caseworker challenged her about being a working mom and stated that she needed to have her priorities straight. The caseworker asked if the older girls "push her buttons," and in court, the report was written stating that the girls "push her buttons" even though Mom had stated that she does not react to them more strongly than any other parent would. CPS distorted and labeled Mom's behavior so that it sounded like she was always yelling and screaming because the girls would always "push her buttons." According to Mom, the presentation to the court was very distorted.

Mom was at work, CPS always knew where to reach her, but they would always show up at home and leave their business cards. The case was then transferred to another caseworker, and over the two years that the case was open, there were three caseworkers.

There was a child therapist involved, and their son, age five, reported that his father had hit him. The therapist met her obligation by reporting this to CPS. The first worker got back involved in the case and "brushed it off." The father stated to the caseworker that he would never do this, and the caseworker believed him. The father also stated to CPS that the mother hit the older girls. The girls had turned against the mom at this point in order to remain loyal to their father, and they confirmed the physical abuse. Mom had to vacate the home. The father at this point was given temporary sole custody, and she got to see the younger kids for supervised visits with her mom supervising.

CPS, despite the income restrictions of the family, stated that the mom had to find a three-bedroom home because she had a boy and a girl, and they could not sleep in the same room or in her room. The kids could stay with their maternal grandmother while mom worked a few hours on Saturday, but their dad insisted that the little ones (ages four and five) be transported almost one hour in each direction so they could be with him while she worked. The transport in mom's opinion became very stressful for the kids.

The caseworker also challenged the mom about how the kids hugged her at ages four and five, stating that it was "too affection-ate." At another point in time, the caseworker told the mom in front of the children that the dad, who was supposed to let her know the whereabouts of the kids when they were with him, did not have to follow this rule as he had temporary sole custody. On another occasion, the caseworker stated to Mom in front of all four children, "You should change the way you walk because you look like you're hiding something."

Her son also said at one point in time that the caseworker had told him, "You have the meanest mommy in the world." Initially the caseworker pressed the fact that Mom had to sign forms about the kids (without an attorney present), or it would adversely affect the kids. At the same meeting, the caseworker stated directly and unprofessionally to the mom, "I don't like you!"

Mom knew she had to go to trial based on the allegations of abuse. (At this point, the mom had legal representation). The night before trial, CPS reversed the substantiation and did not want to take it to trial because there were too many inconsistencies. (It appeared that the hurt of losing her mom, the hurt of the oldest child not getting the attention from this mom as her coach, and the loyalty to their dad over their stepmother led to lying.)

The parents now have joint legal and physical custody of the two younger children. She no longer sees the older girls, and physical custody and parenting time are exchanged by the parents for the younger children.

PART IV

What Can Be Done to Bring About Change

CHAPTER 22

THIS HAS BEEN AN IN-DEPTH look at the hopes and disappointments related to disenfranchised populations and their ability to be in a better position than they are now. I have discussed special education and Child Protective Services and the challenges they face in providing services to individuals and families they are designed to assist. The financial resources needed to provide effective services are not always there. Fortunately for some, the school districts in more affluent areas can provide more, and when this does not happen, those parents who have the funds can fight unfair practices when dealing either with their school district or with Child Protective Services, and the outcomes can be more positive. This is less the case in the inner cities, rural areas, etc., where the level of impoverishment makes it far more difficult to have the funds to fight an unfair decision.

As should not be surprising, money and politics have played key roles in how this has unfolded. The key issues explored involve the fact that the biggest wave of liberalism in the establishment of social service programs and the legislation to enforce it came on the heels of desegregation as the law of the land. In 1954, *Brown v. Board of Education* was the Supreme Court case that forever changed the face of education. As a result of this court case, desegregation of public schools was required by law. As is always the case when any new law is enforced, not everyone will be on board. In the case of desegregation, especially in the Southern states, a long history of segregation of blacks would not easily give way to change, and this led to tremendous protest among those whose rights were violated by the new law and those people who were sympathetic to their plight.

It is always true in the United States that immigration has led to various groups who would not get a fair shake when first coming to America. People would often come to this country with limited job skills, limited command of the English language, and no particular place to settle. It would often be that with this combination of factors, they might move in with family, and various ethnic groups would settle in a particular area of the country and bring their culture and customs with them. This process of immigration to the United States has always been part of the fabric of our culture.

Over time, people would save money, perhaps move, and at the very least, be better off than when they first came. The fact that people can move freely, express themselves, have access to their own cultural and religious experiences has made this country the land of opportunity and also a melting pot where cultures would blend, customs would be shared, and people who settle here would ultimately assimilate into the larger culture of the United States.

The points made in this book and elsewhere are that some barriers to assimilation make it more difficult to move forward than others. It is certainly true that the only group of people who came to this country against their will were slaves from Africa, and their subservience over so many years in bondage has caused untold damage psychologically, which has been documented in particular by black authors, and in this book, I have discussed the work of Dr. Kenneth B. Clark in particular. It is also true that although this country has painted itself as "the land of the free and the home of the brave," there have been horrible miscarriages of justice related to this core set of values including our attacks on Native Americans and their confinement to reservations in several areas of the country. Japanese people during World War II were confined to internment camps in California. In terms of those who do not speak the language, there are often jokes told about Mexicans who cannot speak English, comments about other groups particularly those who speak Spanish where the comments often stated directly in front of those from that group going something like this: "If they want to come to this country, they need to learn to speak our language!"

It is certainly true as well that people confined to a wheelchair, are blind, hearing impaired, or cognitively impaired are not understood by groups without these barriers, and laws have been passed to try to create better opportunities for these individuals, such as ramps for wheelchairs, braille number boards in elevators, etc. Even these relatively simple changes were not easy to obtain for many years.

In the period from 1960 to 1975, John F. Kennedy as president and Robert F. Kennedy as attorney general began to conceptualize the ideas of enforcement of the rights of the disenfranchised. It was politically the right time, and there were clear pressures for enforcement. The court decision to desegregate in 1954 led to protests, which began to happen when these rights were not enforced, especially in the Southern states. The Freedom Riders were a group both white and black who came to the South to rebel. Quietly and not by force, they would walk into a lunch counter and sit down and challenge the police to move them when blacks and whites would sit together at the same lunch counter. This sparked protests throughout the South, including the bus boycotts, which began shortly after a tired woman, Rosa Parks, could only find a seat in the white section of the bus she was on and challenged old principles of segregation.

Martin Luther King Jr. picked up the reins of this protest movement and organized peaceful bus boycotts throughout the Southern states. However, the more threatening these groups became, the more violent the reaction by the local police and, as time progressed, the National Guard. The riots in Harlem, Watts, Newark, and Chicago followed as the disenfranchised openly expressed their anger and began to model a more violent approach, which was supported by a psychiatrist by the name of Frantz Fanon and the head of the Black Muslims, Malcolm X. This level of violence only threatened the white power structure even more.

It was hoped that the liberal presidency of Lyndon B. Johnson (with respect to social empowerment) would allow solutions to emerge from the affected communities and, after the assassination of Kennedy, that Johnson and Robert Kennedy would join forces and bring about true social change. However, an acrimonious relationship between the two made it impossible for them to work together.

Johnson fought for and passed through Congress an enormous amount of civil rights legislation during 1964–1965, and funds were to be distributed to local community action boards, allowing for maximum feasible participation of community leaders to target the problem areas and generate solutions. However, the founding fathers of these types of programs, most notably Dr. Kenneth B. Clark, who had coordinated the expert witness testimony in *Brown v. Board of Education* and went on to initiate one of the largest and sweeping community action programs in the nation in Harlem, New York.

This program named Haryou (Harlem Youth Opportunities Unlimited) allowed for preschool education programs, job programs, mental health services, etc. Sweeping programs started to address housing and urban renewal and upgrading education and the living situations of many disenfranchised families in the inner city.

However, politics once again reared its ugly head, because in Harlem was a power broker, the Reverend Adam Clayton Powell Jr., who was not about to give up his power base to the people in the community who were inexperienced, undertrained yet threatening to the existing order. He persuaded Dr. Clark to merge Haryou with his community service program ACT, and as Powell was chairman of the committee that provided the funding through Congress, although skeptical, Clark had few choices but to comply with Powell's political maneuvering. Believing that he could enlist the help of Robert Kennedy and his staff to force Powell to back down, Clark was sadly disappointed that Kennedy would not lift a finger to help him as he at first had a run for and won the senate seat for New York and later in the decade ran for president, and he could not afford to alienate a powerful congressman in his state.

Throughout the United States, similar political wrangling with the federal government and the likes of Mayor Richard Daley of Chicago meant that these community action programs were underfunded and never given the power needed to make a difference. However, based on my experiences over the last forty years, even if the community action groups were fully funded, they would have inevitably failed because (a) politicians would still have fought them at every turn and (b) their level of inexperience would have led to failure and the tendency for government to swoop in and pick up the pieces after they failed. This happened on a small level as financial improprieties, problems with bookkeeping and record keeping constituted the early days of Haryou, and the program was subsequently investigated by the government for these infractions.

Although honored by his peers when elected to the presidency of the American Psychological Association, Clark was bitter at this point as his dream had been shattered by the political process. Parallel to this process, disenfranchised groups such as the cognitively impaired were brought into the limelight by investigative exposés, such as the case against Willowbrook, an institution for the cognitively impaired who forced its residents to live in this institution in Staten Island in squalid and horrendous conditions. Geraldo Rivera, a newscaster, brought this story into the public light, and it was picked up by one of the causes initiated by Robert Kennedy, who by then was senator from New York, and this is based on his own history of having an institutionalized sister and being sensitive to these issues because of this.

As illustrated earlier in this book, other parents picked up the ball, and in Pennsylvania, the Pennsylvania Association of Retarded Citizens (PARC) initiated a class action suit against the Commonwealth of Pennsylvania, leading to a consent decree where due process was extended to parents to fight on behalf of their loved ones for better conditions and a chance at education in the public schools in the Commonwealth.

Sadly, it became all too clear that the political wrangling would never give true control over to any citizens group. As a result, all programs aimed to help the inner city and to help the public schools were never fully funded, and as a result, the most experienced people were not given the opportunity or the money to run these programs properly.

What came out of the community action movement is a new black middle class. Those who could went on to college (the easy-to-reach poor), and they received a huge number of jobs working in the state and federal government with the newly formed social service programs. They lacked experience and the money to do their job properly. This extended to other disenfranchised groups, such as Latin Americans who were prized because of their bilingualism, which could be utilized to allow the population of Hispanic people in the local community who needed services to speak to someone who might have come from the same life experiences, but if not, certainly spoke the language.

They were left adrift, however, because these individuals had neither the power nor the money to succeed. Further, there was a period where businesses, social service programs, and the like would actually pay for further training and, in some cases, the tuition for advanced degrees. However, in New York City, for example, although open enrollment led to people being admitted to college, those who entered often had a poor fundamental education and could not make it through college, and the expense base of free tuition that was provided by the City of New York changed so that there would be tuition fees, making it harder to continue. This is even worse throughout the country as escalating college costs made it prohibitive for many to go on for advanced schooling.

I was fortunate, however, having attended City College when free tuition was still available, and when I attended Penn State, a graduate assistantship paid my tuition while I engaged in work on a federal grant. The thing is, the training I was offered left me much of the time on my own. People could provide advisement, but I had to learn while doing. As I entered Penn State, it was the first year that IEPs became enforced as documents required to monitor the progress of each handicapped student. There really was less training available than should have been the case, and with such an important piece of legislation yielding the production of IEPs for each student and parent involvement with their child's special education, we did not even know what an IEP was, and we had to "wing it." It was worse for those who followed me and those who did not have the opportunities for the education I was fortunate to receive.

CHAPTER 23

Based on my own background, historical perspectives, and case studies, I have illustrated the pitfalls in special education and social services provision with greatest focus on the problems in the inner city. I have also delineated that the problems I have experienced and have talked about here are embedded in a political reality that made the efforts to provide the best possible services doomed to only partially succeed and sometimes fail miserably under the current political system.

Based on my experiences, I have concluded that under the current political system, which provides both special education services and social services, programming people who provide these services will continue to be undertrained and underfunded (in the area of special education services training to teach a particular population is often good, but the flexibility to understand all the ramifications of one's decisions and even more concerning the way child study teams serve as gatekeepers to special education rather than as problem solvers), and there are ways to better solve this in my opinion.

The successful programs I have discussed reached a level of success due to the fact that the people in those cases who administered the services were better trained and funding was made available without the levels of strict controls that tend to suffocate such programs. For example, one of the programs I had worked for had their own funding efforts, which led to more available money than could be offered only through state auspices (i.e., private funding to at least supplement state funding is one way).

Even in areas where such success is possible, the programs seem to not be able to get away from the pitfalls that strangle social service programs. For example, one residential treatment program that I worked for funded me with a stipend from their own budget to supplement the payment of client counseling services through Medicaid. This arrangement allowed them to have a more highly trained person continue to work because they had no expectation that I would work for them for the little that Medicaid paid per client. However, managed care reared its ugly head, which is the process of cost cutting medical and psychological services, and a nearby hospital actually "bought out" the clinical services being provided at this institution. I was originally hired to work temporarily for only six months for this agency, and my work was so admired that I continued with the program for two and a half years. At the time the clinical services were bought out, the clinical director swore up and down that it would not affect my position. I found out soon after this that they could no longer fund my position and I was being let go.

At this time, a young social worker with whom I had a good relationship called me to let me know that it appeared that everything would work out fine for her, and soon after that she called me back crying and stated that she too had been let go due to lack of funding.

I am aware as well of one school for students with emotional problems (not acting out individuals but students with anxiety, depression, and other emotional issues), and they are not approved as a state-approved private school by design. If they accepted students as a state-approved school, they would be forced to accept many acting-out students, and their philosophy is that it would ruin the integrity of the program.

I also discussed a Head Start Program I worked for in central Pennsylvania. This became a tremendous success due to the actions of the director. What made it a success is that he fought with the head of the community action program, and the Head Start Program was ultimately made an independent freestanding entity no longer under the control of the community action program. Again, if the money flows directly into a program without the administrative constraints and financial constraints that happen when under the same level of direct government control—meaning in this case, money siphoned into a whole array of programs, some successful and some unsuccessful—the program is more likely to grow and prosper.

The last program I worked for that has been a tremendous success is the school for the neurologically impaired, where its budget was expanded beyond funding of the state and federal government due to private fund-raising efforts on the part of the school's visionary founder. This school went on to become a Blue Ribbon School, which means that the federal government went on to honor the school as an exemplary program. The value of the staff was also made clear, as each of us received a watch embossed with the name of the school and the accolade Blue Ribbon School on the face of the watch, honoring each staff member for their contribution to this honor.

However, Child Protective Services and the schools in the inner city remain fixed and dilated as entities of the state, which will not change anytime soon unless the financial structure and the power given to well-trained staff allow for good decisions on behalf of the population they serve.

How can this be accomplished? you ask. The answer from my point of view is that private funding needs to become involved in either formulating independent programs or supplementing current costs that are paid by the government. The amount of funding made available currently will never be enough to do this job.

There are many things that can be done to accomplish this task. There has been a long history of private funds being made available for social service programs and education. The most visible model today of alternative ways to provide funding is the charter school. This has a mixed history, as in some cases, the funding is made available, which allows more well-trained staff to be hired, as wells as programming, which can work to improve each students capacity to learn and to be motivated to learn. However, there are many charter schools that are woefully underfunded.

The best role model I can think of, although on a smaller level than I am imagining, is St. Jude Children's Research Hospital. The hospital was founded by Danny Thomas, a well-known comedian and TV star. I am sure in the early days, because of his connection with the entertainment industry, many from that industry donated funds to get this off the ground. There is currently an active funding effort where it has become a charitable contribution, and Marlo Thomas, the daughter of Danny Thomas (who is an actress in her own right), has continued the fund-raising efforts for this hospital.

The unique thing about this hospital is that it started on the premise that there are seriously ill children whose families are not receiving the funds they need to help their child get better. Through St. Jude, children are seen, their families are given money for lodging, food and their child's medical care are covered, and for all these services, the family never receives a bill. Similarly, Ronald McDonald House, which is set up through McDonald's, provides lodging at these houses near hospitals caring for sick children. I am not familiar with all that they do, but the idea is certainly along similar lines. The point is that there is tremendous wealth in the entertainment industry and corporations like McDonald's, and we as a society, through this process and private donations by the general population, can even do better. We as a society can be better than this, but the political process leaves a lot to be desired in this day and age.

One of the interesting things that cannot be ignored in raising these issues is the way in which typically, in my experience, money is raised for social programs and educational programs when conducted on a large scale. The imprint goes back many years to the efforts of Jerry Lewis and fund-raising through an entertainment packed telethon each Labor Day on behalf of muscular dystrophy. I am in no way taking issue with the sizable amount of money raised for this very worthy cause. However, the methods have been challenged before, and with what I am suggesting, it is imperative to say things as they are to get my point across and force people to think.

The kids on the Telethon were less presented for what they can do than by trying to raise the sympathy of the public to donate money. It was very effective at that time, but we have to reexamine why this is necessary. At that time, in the climate we lived in and when the effort was started, it was way before the big push for special education of even the most severely disabled, as I have discussed in this book. At that time, I accept the fact that there may have been no other way to get donations. I have to believe we have come a long way and, further, that we have a long way to go but in this country are up to the task.

More recent commercials I have seen for St. Jude, for example, are more positive and upbeat, but it must be said that we as a society have liked to contribute money when other people are in a one-down position and cannot hurt us in any way, i.e., children who are ill and orphans or starving children overseas.

What I am talking about is completely different, because of the belief system of many about what could happen if. I mean this to say that in addition to racial prejudice, after the issues with riots, Black Muslims, shooting police, etc., it is only recently that the flip side is being examined with the rush of black individuals who are attacked and sometimes for no reason other than skin color and hurt, killed, or worse. As stated earlier, it is also dangerous for police in these neighborhoods, and I am not undermining the fact that there are two sides. However, to contribute money to try to better the social services or education in poor neighborhoods, when the public who are not in this situation would like to believe that as a group, these people are lowlifes and downright dangerous, is asking for a great deal of change in attitude. As stated by Dr. Kenneth Clark and as I am stating now, the inner city can completely destroy one's motivation and spirit if you grow up in such surroundings, and the money has to be handled the right way. Dr. Clark was an eminent professor, yet a politician (Adam Clayton Powell), as stated earlier, was to make sure he did not become that powerful in "his neighborhood" (Harlem). Come on, folks, if history is to allow us to learn from our mistakes, let's learn!

It was ridiculous as also stated earlier in the book to give money to gang members and expect them to use it to clean up their neighborhoods, but if given to job programs, schools, hospitals, etc., even in the inner city, this is not ridiculous! However, you need to have the money to hire the best people, not just keep putting the undertrained and underfunded to work. We are better than this, and we can do a better job but not through political hands alone. Underfunding will happen over and over again. People can judge and turn a blind eye to the lowlifes and thugs, but take a closer look and you are talking about real people who do not have a great opportunity to get started. Yes, there are some examples of great people coming from the inner city, but unfortunately, this is not the majority.

CHAPTER 24

A MAJOR AREA OF CONCERN as well is how money is to be utilized. Sadly, for many years, when dealing with children, the bulk of money in social services at any community level is provided to teenagers. They are the ones who are the more likely to act out, commit crimes, use drugs, etc. However, it is true that starting with the very youngest can yield big outcomes before "the damage is done." Again, I am in no way suggesting that money should be removed from programs for teenagers, but often, when I have raised the issue in any community why there are so few programs for young children, the response will often be, "We don't have the money."

The younger you start, the more successful the outcome. It is clear that of all the social service initiatives started during the War on Poverty, the most popular, without doubt, was Head Start. The more you can do for preschoolers and those who are in the beginning years of elementary school, the bigger the payoff. Younger students are far more receptive to being led toward a more vibrant and solid education than those whose self-esteem and motivation to learn have already been affected by the emotional starvation and educational starvation suffered in the current system at the hands of bureaucrats.

Secondly, the monies need to flow to those who are also working with the local universities and social research facilities. One of the points made earlier in the book about the War on Poverty is that money was spent without being adequately researched. What I found to be most invaluable when I worked for Head Start is the fact that I had channels of communication with Penn State University and could ask and receive answers about things I was just learning about, and I had the opportunity to share this information with the leaders of the program. Thirdly, universities are far more equipped when provided with funds to conduct research on the efficacy of such programs. This was true when I was on a federal grant providing services to the Multiply Handicapped Education Project, which was researched as we proceeded over the three years the grant was in existence. This was clearly the intent of Dr. Kenneth B. Clark, but his efforts fell at the hands of politicians who were threatened by this approach and the effect that it would have on the existing power base in Harlem.

Fourth, there is a process of gentrification happening in Harlem and other ghettos around the United States. People are moving in and creating better housing, but they are not giving anything back. If one wants to have housing at a cheaper rate, those people should have the obligation of offering their time or their money in other ways to help the community grow and thrive. This may sound somewhat communal, but what of it?

Although on a much smaller scale compared with the federal government, the people at Ben and Jerry's who were 1960s thinkers set up a thriving ice cream business in Vermont, which became a large national company by providing for its workers in that the workers have a financial stake in the company. We can certainly take a page out of this playbook and try to run with it.

Fifth, the most skilled people can contribute some of their time to the fledgling social services and educational programs. Doctors without Borders have sent doctors and dentists into impoverished countries to provide medical and dental services, and the same thing can be done here at home. If they offer training to local professionals who remain in the community, they will certainly upgrade the level of services offered. By the same token, financial incentives have been offered to doctors especially to settle in more rural communities to upgrade the services. Just like I was offered a stipend to supplement Medicaid payments, private fund-raising can raise the money to try this.

Sixth, there is a current move toward prison reform. Privatizing the prisons or privatizing schools is currently in process. This is excellent, except the goal cannot always be about making the best profit as compared with funding the best services. It is excellent to try to implement services, such as providing drug rehab services to those who commit minor offenses that are drug related rather than placing these individuals in prison cells. These are all programs that can be tried but need to stand the test of time and have the money to function properly.

As stated earlier, all such programs should have a university affiliation, and the funds should flow to those people in the various areas of service delivery with the most training. Research should be conducted on the efficacy of these programs before continuing to throw money at it. Finally, as is typical of our capitalist system, private bidding can take place with the funding going to the university and program that provides the best financial package and is assessed to be the best program for the area.

These are just a few of the myriad of ideas that can be tried to turn both special education and social service programming around. It is my hope that this book will stimulate thought by the public who read this book and that this will generate many more ideas on our path to better successes than we are seeing today.

REFERENCES

Guerney, L. F. (2014). *Parenting: A skills training manual* (6th ed.). North Bethesda, MD: IDEALS.

King, S. (1983). *Pet sematary.* Garden City, NY: Doubleday.

Lemann, N. (1988). The unfinished war. *The Atlantic, 262*(6). Retrieved from http://www.theatlantic.com/past/politics/poverty/lemunf1.htm

Lemann, N. (1989). The unfinished war. *The Atlantic, 263*(1). Retrieved from http://www.theatlantic.com/past/politics/poverty/lemunf2.htm

Matlin, D. (2014). The unknown Kenneth B. Clark. *The Harvard Press Blog.* Retrieved from http://harvardpress.typepad.com/hup-publicity/2014/07/the-unknown-kenneth-b-clark-daniel-matlin.html

Montgomery, P. L. (1964, June 25). Haryou-Act sets $118 million budget. *The New York Times.* Retrieved from http://www.nytimes.com/1964/06/25/haryou-act-sets-118-million-budget.html?r=0

Ortwein, M. (1997). *Mastering the magic of play: A training manual for parents in filial therapy.* Silver Spring, MD: Relationship Press.

Roberts, S. (2015, June 28). Marva Collins, educator who aimed high for poor, black students, dies a 78. *The New York Times.* Retrieved from http://www.nytimes.com/2015/06/29/us/marva-collins-78-no-nonsense-educator-and-activist-dies.html

Schanberg, S. H. (1964, Aug 26). Haryou will get. *The New York Times*. Retrieved from http://www.nytimes.com/1964/08/26/haryou-will-get.html?_r=0

Weistuch, N. M. (1987). *The role of school psychologists in the history of special education in the commonwealth of Pennsylvania (1896-1975)*. (Unpublished doctoral dissertation). Pennsylvania State University, State College, PA.

ABOUT THE AUTHOR

Dr. Norman Weistuch grew up in the Bronx in the 1950s to 1960s and was educated in the public schools during the first wave of desegregation in the city. Educated through his master's degree in school psychology at the City College of New York, he was exposed to a professor while an undergraduate student Dr. Kenneth B. Clark, who was the prime witness in the *Brown v. Board of Education* case in 1954 that led to desegregation of the public schools. Dr. Clark was noteworthy in attempting to bring large amounts of money through his nonprofit Haryou to the Harlem community with disappointing results.

This thinking has had a profound effect on the author, who continued his education through his PhD in school psychology at the Pennsylvania State University. After working for a Head Start Program in Pennsylvania, Dr. Weistuch moved to New Jersey and has worked for numerous school districts and special school programs and developed a private practice in Princeton, New Jersey. In addition to advocating with families having issues with their local school districts about special education placements, Dr. Weistuch also spent several years consulting for Child Protective Services in that state. He has experienced great disillusionment about the process of providing sound clinical and school-related services in both the special education arena and the arena involving child protection, and he has interviewed parents and offered suggestions about how to make things better.

CPSIA information can be obtained
at www.ICGtesting.com
Printed in the USA
BVOW03s1814120617
486693BV00001B/15/P